"So you're admitting that you wanted to be stranded with me?"

Clare sighed, knowing that she was doing a horrible job of this. "Not stranded with you in a romantic setting but more stranded on an island where mob bosses and their cheerful thugs can't get to me. I heard you say during the party that you were going to be sailing around, or whatever the hell you call it, for the next couple of weeks or so. That's the reason I stowed away."

That distrustful look was back in his eyes again. Not that she could blame him. Frustration and that familiar resentment sat like a boulder on Clare's chest. She'd slogged for so many years, carefully building her life so that she didn't need anyone in it. With one move, her father had negated everything she'd achieved. She was going to sound ridiculous for saying what she was about to say.

"Explain, now," Dev said, in a hard tone that did wonders for the quagmire of self-pity that was threatening to engulf her. "And no more beating about the bush. Give it to me straight."

"Straight, right. Here goes... I'd like you to kidnap me."

Signed, Sealed...Seduced

Billion-dollar deals and breathtaking passion!

At boarding school, Clare, Bea and Amy formed an unbreakable bond. Years later, they're making waves as the owners of their own successful PR company. But having billionaires for clients means the most unexpected tasks...and *temptation*...can be thrown in their paths at a moment's notice!

Amy is sent to the Mediterranean kingdom of Vallia by the unusual request to ruin King Luca's image. What she doesn't expect is to be the center of the scandal!

Read more in
Ways to Ruin a Royal Reputation by Dani Collins

Shy Bea is left alone to handle their most important client, Ares! First job: accompany him to a Venetian ball...

Find out more in
Cinderella's Night in Venice by Clare Connelly

After escaping from criminals, Clare stows away on tycoon Dev's yacht. When he finds her, they have a convenient deal to strike!

Discover more in
The Playboy's "I Do" Deal by Tara Pammi

Tara Pammi

———

THE PLAYBOY'S "I DO" DEAL

Special thanks and acknowledgment are given to
Tara Pammi for her contribution to the
Signed, Sealed…Seduced miniseries.

HARLEQUIN®
PRESENTS®

ISBN-13: 978-1-335-40371-1

The Playboy's "I Do" Deal

Copyright © 2021 by Harlequin Books S.A.

This edition published by arrangement with Harlequin Books S.A.

For questions and comments about the quality of this book,
please contact us at CustomerService@Harlequin.com.

Harlequin Enterprises ULC
22 Adelaide St. West, 40th Floor
Toronto, Ontario M5H 4E3, Canada
www.Harlequin.com

Printed in U.S.A.

Tara Pammi can't remember a moment when she wasn't lost in a book—especially a romance, which was much more exciting than a mathematics textbook at school. Years later, Tara's wild imagination and love for the written word revealed what she really wanted to do. Now she pairs alpha males who think they know everything with strong women who knock that theory and them off their feet!

Books by Tara Pammi

Harlequin Presents

Born into Bollywood

Claiming His Bollywood Cinderella
The Surprise Bollywood Baby

Conveniently Wed!

Sicilian's Bride for a Price

Once Upon a Temptation

The Flaw in His Marriage Plan

The Scandalous Brunetti Brothers

An Innocent to Tame the Italian
A Deal to Carry the Italian's Heir

Visit the Author Profile page
at Harlequin.com for more titles.

CHAPTER ONE

HIDING OUT FROM thugs who'd kidnap her in a heartbeat and cart her off to marry some beer-bellied, gold-toothed creepy old man who gave out loans in exchange for *desirable assets* wasn't how Clare Roberts had imagined her life playing out.

Not even as a girl with the extraordinary imagination that had been needed for transforming her feckless father, who'd dumped her at her unwilling aunt's doorstep when she'd been five, into an emotionally available superhero for years.

But just when she thought she'd hit rock-bottom, life decided to show her the green icky stuff beneath the nasty pond scum.

Desirable asset...the very phrase made her want to throw up.

To escape Goon Number One, who had made it clear he'd collect her instead of the money she owed his Mob boss—because when her dad had borrowed money from them he'd used *her* as collateral and then died before he could pay it back—the only option left to her was hiding out on board the superyacht of the man she'd slept with not a month ago. While the night had been everything she'd hoped for and more, the morning after had been entirely too awkward. Her one-night stand had neatly deleted her from his life as easily as spam email.

Served her right for taking an imprudent dive into the roller-coaster world of sex and romance with CEO and unapologetic bachelor playboy Dev Kohli. A former gold-medal-winning swimmer who had gone on to create the world's most contemporary sports brand Athleta. A billionaire before he'd turned thirty and a self-made man, the latter quality being something Clare had admired enormously for a long time after she'd first met him at a PR event she'd organized for one of his friends. As well as his wide shoulders and rock-hard abs, that was.

She should've known her own PR company, The London Connection, might do business with him in the future. After all, he was a man who was reputed to be more loyal to his clients than his lovers.

While Clare completely agreed with the sentiment for a business-only relationship, it pricked a little when, as an ex-lover, one fell into the former category. Not that she was still moping after him.

But the heart wanted what it wanted…or in her case, it was her lady bits that had done all the wanting, after being firmly denied until the ripe old age of twenty-eight.

A hysterical giggle—fueled by the two glasses of champagne she'd guzzled in panic—escaped her mouth. Her two best friends and business partners Amy and Bea would've teased her no end if she'd said "lady bits" within their hearing. Well, Amy definitely would. Bea would've simply fallen into giggles. But they were both on the other side of the world at that moment, trying to keep their business afloat. Apart from the odd text, they'd hardly heard from one another recently.

God, she missed them like an ache in her champagne-sloshed belly. Desperately wanted to hear at least one of their voices. Tell them what her dad had done to her and then have a cry while they cursed him to hell and back. He'd known he was dying and had sent her money to start The London Connection, which had gone from strength to strength in the last two years. He'd only lived for days afterward, and she hadn't even fully processed what it meant to discover now that, far from thinking her father had finally done something good for her, he'd actually betrayed her in the worst possible way, just to salve his own conscience for having ignored her for her whole life.

But contacting them while she was on the run from a mobster who was intent on kidnapping her and dragging her off to his cave was definitely not a good idea. What if he threatened Amy or Bea because he couldn't locate Clare? After all, anyone who'd done even a bit of digging into her life would know Amy and Bea were her true family. The only people who cared about her in the whole wide world.

No, she couldn't take the risk of endangering their lives too. So she'd decided it was better for them if neither of knew where she was—or who she was with. Her friends knew how determined she could be when she was on the scent of a new client, so she figured that when they didn't hear from her for a while, that's what they'd assume she was doing.

What her friends also didn't know, and Clare wasn't about to tell them, was that their new client was the same man she'd had a one-night stand with recently. She'd never shared his identity with them, feeling a strange sense of protectiveness about that night. Also, because if she talked to them, then she'd have to own up that she'd mostly failed at abiding by the most important rule of one-night stands—keeping it strictly casual. Especially as Dev had clearly had no such problem doing that himself.

Athleta was far too big a fish for Clare to walk away from just because its CEO hadn't proclaimed that he'd love her forever. And tonight had been her one chance to impress on him that her small PR firm could clean up his recently tarnished image.

Only the mobster's goons had trailed her all the way from London to a conference in New York and then to São Paulo, and it was terrifying. Today the mobster's intentions had been made crystal clear. He intended to simply...*take* her in lieu of the money he insisted she owed him.

For two weeks, she'd lived in terror of being snatched from wherever she was.

She'd been meaning to hightail it back to her hotel room when she'd spotted Goon Number One with a drink in hand on the main deck of the superyacht this evening. The short, blond, chubby-faced man had smiled angelically—clearly his cheerful appearance was a useful tool in nabbing unsuspecting women. It was the same man she'd seen leaning near the newspaper stand on the street where The London Connection's offices were located, looking up at the sole window. The very same posh and supposedly secure street that they paid astronomical rent for.

He'd even bumped into her late one evening when she'd been rushing to catch the Tube after work. Apologized profusely. When she'd then seen him lounging in the foyer of her New York hotel, she'd wondered if she was hallucinating.

Now, he was here, aboard Dev's yacht. Looking just as posh as the rest of the designer-suited men. Wearing an affable smile, chitchatting away.

He'd almost touched her. Tried to talk to her as if they were long-lost friends. She didn't have time to wonder how he'd got on board. She needed to hide. Now.

She ran her hand over her hips, contemplating the rounds the uniformed security guard was making. The emerald green silk skirt she was wearing had been a gift from Bea, and it gave her some much-needed courage. Without looking back, she stepped gingerly down the spiral staircase—who knew yachts could have staircases like this one?—and tried to not trip in her four-inch heels.

The champagne sloshed around in her belly again as she passed door after door. Peeked into one expansive lounge after another. Even in her panic, Clare couldn't help marveling at the airy, contemporary spaces, the chic stylish interiors. The click-click of her stilettos on the gleaming floors sounded like a sinister countdown.

Heart pounding, she walked into the biggest cabin. For a second, she was thrown at the sheer size of it. A large bed with a navy-blue duvet looked so welcoming that she took an involuntary step toward it longingly.

It was the feel of the luxuriously soft cotton underneath her fingertips that made her realize she was pawing it. Her eyelids felt heavy, her entire body swooning with exhaustion. She'd been traveling nonstop for a week. Hadn't slept a wink ever since that ghastly man had started following her. But she couldn't sleep now. Not if she wanted to remain undetected until after the party wound down.

After one last wistful glance at the bed, she shook off the lethargic fog that threatened to engulf her. She was crashing from the shock of seeing that mobster's henchman again. Moving like an automaton, she walked into a massive closet.

It was about the size of her bedroom at her tiny flat. A faint scent of sandalwood and something else reached her nostrils. Her belly swooped, with a more pleasurable sensation this time. The memory of Dev's hard body driving into hers, the feel of the taut, sweat-slicked skin of his back under her greedy fingers... Clare couldn't help but cling to the memory of the utter feeling of ecstasy he'd brought her to. That moment of sheer intimacy when he'd looked into her eyes and simply...*seen* her. All of her vulnerability displayed on her face. And he'd just held her tenderly and kissed her temple.

The sense of well-being that arose from that memory suddenly calmed the fear brewing in her belly.

She sat down in the vast window seat and looked at the ocean. The expanse of blue was a symbol of how far away she was from her home, her friends and the business she'd built up with her own blood, sweat and tears.

But also on the other side of it was the man who claimed he owned her as if she were cattle.

Clare kicked off her heeled sandals and pulled her knees up to her chest. Leaning back against the plush upholstery, she closed her eyes and waited for her heart to slow its pounding beat.

For the party to be over.

For the yacht to start moving.

Every inch of her rebelled at the idea of traveling to a destination unknown with a man who'd walked away from her without a backward glance after the best night of her life. Who'd told her in no uncertain terms that while it had been pleasurable, their...association was over.

But the billionaire playboy meant safety for now. Even if that meant she'd be clinging to him like an unwanted piece of flotsam.

"Promise me you'll make it to the wedding, Dev. Please."

Dev Kohli pressed a long finger to his throbbing temple, his mild headache becoming aggravated by his twin sister's shrill pleading.

But since Dev didn't lie to himself—it was the only way he'd been able to survive in the military school environment his father had placed him in—he acknowledged that it was guilt that was turning one of the worst months of his life into something much...worse.

"You haven't even met Richard. I mean, Rich

and I've been engaged for eight months and my twin brother hasn't met him yet. That's a bit much, even for you, Dev. Don't you want to make sure…"

Diya went on, without needing any more response from him than his grunts peppered throughout the conversation.

The fact that his sister—younger than him by a whole two and a half minutes—was piling on the guilt didn't mean that it was unwarranted.

He hadn't been back to his family's home in California since military school. He hadn't seen Diya in eighteen months. But, even throughout the nearly two-decades-long rift he and Papa had sustained, he'd always made it a priority to see his siblings. Even if all his attorney general older brother and renowned pediatric neurosurgeon older sister did was try to talk him into coming home.

It was Diya who had always been the one to check on him. Even when he'd turned his back on all the rest of them, Diya had been his only connection to his roots. His estranged family. To the one person he'd loved and lost—their mama.

"When's the wedding?" Dev asked, just to interrupt the barrage of English and Hindi building up momentum, spewing at him from across the Atlantic. He'd stared at the date for long enough in the last few weeks.

"You know exactly when it is," Diya snapped.

"This isn't the right time for me to visit California, Diya," he explained softly. "You know what I've been facing in the media. This sexual harassment scandal that's threatening my company's name is not a trivial matter.

"I've got people working around the clock to make sure something like that never happens again. And if I show my face at the wedding right in the middle of this…messy scandal, you know what *he* will say."

His sister didn't need to ask who "he" was.

"The last thing I need right now is to hear his negative voice preaching at me," Dev said, bitter even now. After all these years. Even after he'd proved his despotic father wrong on so many fronts.

"Dev, you can't let the past—"

"I just don't have the bandwidth to sit through another episode of family drama. If I stay far enough away, we can continue to pretend that we're the embodiment of the wealthy, successful Indian American family he's always wanted to be. Do you want to have your wedding upstaged by one of our dirty fights?"

Diya sighed. "If I have to spend every minute leading up to the ceremony keeping you and Papa apart, then I'll do it. In fact, I'll recruit Richard to play referee between you two. Papa adores Richard."

That little fact came at him like a bolt he hadn't

even seen coming, lodging painfully in his chest. Dev wanted to bang his cell phone against the glittering glass bar and forget all about the wedding. Of course, his father approved of Diya's investment banker fiancé.

And at twenty-nine, here he was, still envious of something a stranger had—his father's admiration. As if he was that pathetic twelve-year-old boy again, desperate to please his father and utterly failing.

"I'm so sorry, Dev."

Dev sighed. "Not your fault, D."

No one understood how deep the scars of his childhood were, not even Diya. Not his obediently perfect older brother or his genius older sister either. It was like they'd had a father different from the one he'd been given.

Sometimes, he resented them all so much. But mostly for expecting him to just…get over it. To forget that he'd always felt like an outsider among his famous family's overachieving members. Especially after Mama had died.

No, he'd been made to feel like that. By Papa. Until he'd been sent away to the military school at twelve—which had turned out to be a blessing in disguise—Dev had been yelled at by his father, bullied into believing that he was nothing. That he was a cuckoo in a crow's nest.

And that was something he could neither forgive nor forget.

"I promise you, Dev," Diya said, launching into dire warnings now, "if you don't show up for my wedding, I'll…forbid you from seeing your future niece or nephew. Cut you out of my life. There will be epic poems written about the estranged uncle." Dev could hear the calming tones of a man speaking in the background, undoubtedly Richard. He smiled, despite the tightness in his chest.

He wondered what kind of a man had willingly signed up for a lifetime with his firecracker of a younger sister.

Damn it, this wasn't how it should be. Him thousands of miles away from his brother and two sisters and nieces and nephews. Mama would've been immensely saddened by this family rift that had left him utterly alone. She'd have wanted so much more for him than this solitary, nomadic lifestyle.

"Let me sort through the mess my company's in right now," Dev said, making up his mind, "and I'll be there at your wedding."

"You know that we all have faith in you, don't you? Whatever those trashy websites said about you knowing that female executive was being harassed… We know you'd have never tolerated something like that." He had no idea how she'd known, but Diya had just said the one thing that Dev had so badly needed to hear.

"Now, clean up the mess, Dev. And show up at

my wedding with your billionaire halo all freshly polished."

Dev smiled.

"Also, it would be awesome if you could bring a date to the wedding."

The sudden image of silky dark brown hair and intelligent blue eyes boldly holding his gaze as he moved inside her was so vivid in his mind that for a moment Dev stayed mute.

Diya whistled. "So you've met someone! Who is she? What does she do? I can't wait to tell Deedi—"

The excited tone of his twin's voice sent alarm bells ringing in his head. "No one out of the ordinary," he muttered, feeling horrible for saying it.

Clare Roberts had been so far out of the ordinary that he hadn't quite recovered yet. He'd tried to tell himself during the last few weeks that she'd been just the same as his usual one-night stands, but he hadn't quite managed to convince himself of that yet.

"Continuing with the *love them and leave them* policy then, huh?"

"Don't push it," he warned her.

Diya giggled. "Fine. It's on your own head when you show up all single and handsome… Seema Auntie's been asking about you."

Dev groaned. Seema Auntie had been Mama's oldest, dearest friend and the most notoriously ambitious matchmaker on both sides of the Atlantic. With a horde of daughters, she regularly embarrassed eligible men without discrimination.

He quickly hung up after promising to update Diya on his plans.

Talking to his twin always left him feeling restless. As if he was back in his unhappy childhood. As if he hadn't achieved enough, conquered enough. As if he still didn't have enough. The feeling had been returning more and more frequently, and now it had been amplified by the man he'd trusted most using and betraying Dev's name in the worst possible way and endangering the company he'd worked so hard to build.

With a sigh, Dev looked around at the stunning sight of his yacht leaving the Port of Santos behind. He been visiting the nearby city of São Paulo, but he never stayed anywhere longer than a month. His sports merchandise was manufactured all over the world, and he preferred not basing himself permanently in one place.

In his heart, he knew he didn't really want to miss Diya's wedding.

Which meant he had no choice but to hasten the mass cleanup he'd already instigated in the company. There was no way he was showing up in front of his father with a harassment scandal weighing him down.

He was going to show up with his halo shining so bright that even Papa would be blinded by it. Preferably with a gorgeous, accomplished woman on his arm to ward off Seema Auntie, at least. As if waiting for the slightest signal, his mind once again instantly conjured the image of the woman he had determinedly pushed aside from his thoughts for the last three weeks.

While their night together had resulted in one of those rare connections that even the cynic in him had noticed, his behavior the morning after had been less than impeccable.

All the toxic rubbish that had been written over the past three weeks about his company and him at the center of it—a billionaire playboy who treated women with less care than he did his luxury toys—stung sharply when he thought of how he'd behaved toward Clare Roberts.

Granted, his company's name had just been plastered all over the media when he'd woken up that morning with *her* wrapped around him. He'd barely untangled her warm limbs before switching on his phone to find hundreds of messages from his PR team and board of directors. The female executive who'd not only been harassed but then hounded into leaving his company, had released an interview that had gone viral overnight.

A disaster of epic proportions had ensued.

Dev couldn't forgive himself for not realizing what had been going on under his very nose. He'd immediately launched an investigation, firing the man responsible for the harassment within twenty-four hours and offering a rehiring package to the female executive. But it was nowhere near enough.

He'd messed up big time.

He'd been so busy with launching the next product, chasing the next billion-dollar deal that he'd been distracted from his responsibilities toward the people who worked for him. It was the one thing Mama had tried to instill in all her four children.

That with privilege and power came responsibilities.

Dev had completely failed in taking care of his employees. He also knew that the solutions he'd already implemented were not enough to save his company's reputation. And that's where Clare Roberts was supposed to come in.

Walking through his empty yacht, he wondered why she'd disappeared tonight without approaching him. Especially after she'd hounded his secretary for an appointment to see him this very evening. When the initial request had come forward that the CEO of the PR firm The London Connection wished to see him, he'd done his own research.

He hadn't exchanged anything beyond first names with her that night. So, it had been a surprise to see that intelligent face stare back at him from her company's website.

For a second, he'd wondered if she meant to prolong their…association. Hot and memorable as it had been, the last thing Dev needed was a passionate affair distracting him. But he had pushed the arrogant assumption away.

The London Connection was a small firm that had made great strides in the last two years. It had a reputation of being one of the foremost, woman-led companies that conducted PR for big brand names. Also well-known for their charitable efforts and female entrepreneur empowerment initiatives.

Dev had instantly known it was the kind of company he needed to reinvigorate Athleta's reputation. Clearly, Clare had seen the potential in the opportunity too.

Then why disappear before he'd even had a chance to greet her?

Why make all the effort to fly to São Paulo from New York, travel out to the Port of Santos where his yacht was moored, and then leave without even speaking to him?

Dev finished his drink and walked into his closet. Thanks to the call with Diya and now this woman not turning up for their meeting, his skin hummed with restlessness. He needed a vigorous swim. Even as a young boy, swimming had helped him work off the frustration he couldn't verbalize to his parents. He had felt free, as if he could communicate with his limbs instead of his words.

As an adolescent carted off to military school,

his athleticism in the pool had been his saving grace.

He discarded his shirt. He was about to grab a towel from the neatly folded pile when he spotted a bright piece of emerald silk fluttering at the back.

He was very sure he didn't own a piece of fabric in that striking color. He also remembered thinking how well the emerald silk highlighted Clare's deliciously round bottom.

Was she here—still aboard his yacht, in his closet?

He walked past the rows and rows of suits and looked down.

Shock held him rooted for a few seconds, followed by a gamut of emotions he couldn't check. Anger, disillusionment, even humor traveled through him, ending in pure disbelief.

What the hell was she doing here?

She was curled up neatly in the window seat, her white handbag clutched to her cheek and completely…asleep. Her hair made a shiny mess around her face. A curly lock blew away from her face every time she exhaled. Her wide, pink mouth—perhaps a little too wide for her small face—was slightly open.

Dev reached out and gently shook her shoulder.

The last thing he needed was a mishap with another woman—even though she was the one invading his privacy and hiding in his damned closet.

Especially a woman he'd slept with…and hadn't been able to get out of his mind.

CHAPTER TWO

IT WAS A lovely dream.

Naughtily lovely and just what she needed to escape the nightmare reality of her life.

It featured a man's taut buttocks—the kind that athletes had—round and hard. The kind that spawned internet memes. The kind that Clare wouldn't mind sinking her teeth into. And thighs that would have no trouble holding her up against a wall making her sex damp with the raw muscular power in them. And, oh, Lord…that nicely defined V of muscles at his groin and the happy trail that lead to it…

Clare was desperate to hold on to the dream. She knew exactly who she was dreaming about.

Dev Kohli of the tight butt and the broad shoulders and the charming grin and the surprisingly kind eyes.

A loud curse and a hand on her shoulder ripped open the flimsy curtain between dream and reality. Clare sat up jerkily. Jarred into wakefulness, her limbs protested, after having been cramped tight into the window seat.

She looked up to discover Dev Kohli staring down at her with murder in his eyes.

Well, not quite murder precisely, but something close to it.

Clare swallowed. Blast it, had she actually fallen asleep in the man's closet? This was so not how she intended for him to find her. She'd meant to wait until the party was over and walk out and present her case to him like a rational woman.

He stepped back from her as if she was demented. And she couldn't really blame him. In quick movements, he grabbed a shirt and slipped it on.

If one could burn of embarrassment, Clare was sure she should be a steaming pile of ash on his lush carpet.

"Would you like to tell me what you're doing here?" Ice had nothing on his voice. "Or should I call security to handle you?"

Clare rubbed her palm over her temples. "I'm so sorry, Mr. Kohli," she muttered, straightening her skirt awkwardly. Her head felt like it was stuffed full of cotton wool and her belly ready to eat itself in hunger. Yet despite that, there was that prickle of awareness under her skin at his nearness.

"Why are you here, *Ms. Roberts*?" he asked, a

wealth of meaning buried in how he said her last name. A little mocking. A lot annoyed.

Clare met his gaze without hesitation. "I promise, I don't usually go about sneaking into men's cabins. I had the most unbelievably horrid day and then I just… I can't believe I fell asleep. I think it was the scent of you that did it," she said, inanely pointing to rows and rows of Armani shirts.

"I have no idea what that means," he said, the scowl not lessening in intensity.

"I was terrified for my life. And the scent of you in here… I think, it lulled me into thinking I was safe. Because it's familiar, you know. After that night…" She flushed and sighed. "I'm making this worse, aren't I?"

"With every tall tale you're spinning to justify this intrusion, yes. Much, much worse."

"I'm not lying."

"I really doubt that."

It was the disdain in his voice that did it. That made her usually even-keel temper explode. "You think a lot of yourself, don't you? You think you're such a *studly stud* that no woman can stop herself from throwing herself at you? That no woman can keep her clothes on or maintain her dignity around you? That we're all falling over ourselves to get at that tightly packed muscular body of yours?"

Damn, girl, she could hear Amy's admiring laughter in her head.

Her face heating, Clare readied herself to be thrown out of the very window where she'd been hiding. It was shock, she told herself. Shock was making her mouth off like this.

Into the stunned silence came his laughter. Deep, low laughter that enveloped Clare like a comfortingly warm blanket. His face had broken into attractive grooves and lines, the flash of his white teeth rendering him even more gorgeous. If that was possible.

She looked away, needing a respite from all his irresistible masculinity. The dark hollow of his throat made her belly somersault. She had a vivid memory of burying her face there when she'd climaxed. And he'd held her afterward, as if she was precious to him.

The taste of his skin—sweat and salt and so deliciously male—practically hovered on her tongue.

Slowly, praying that her thoughts weren't betrayed on her face, Clare met his gaze. There was chagrin and impatience and more than a hint of humor lurking in the brown depths.

"That wasn't what I'd intended to say."

"Clearly. But that's probably the most truthful you've been just now, huh?" he said, agreeing with a grace she wasn't sure she deserved.

Clare couldn't summon a smile. "Just give me a

minute to gather my bearings, please. I'll explain everything properly. And then—" she swallowed the fear "—if you still want to throw me out, you can just toss me into the ocean. It's probably safer for me anyway."

"Two minutes," he said, moving away.

He returned with an opened bottle of sparkling water and Clare took it gratefully. His gaze didn't move from her as she finished the bottle. It wasn't…roguish or obvious but she had a feeling he'd done a thorough sweep of her, from her bare feet to her short dark brown hair, still in disarray.

She fiddled with the empty bottle for a few seconds and then cleared her throat. "I'm not usually this unprofessional. I've had a really bad day, Mr. Kohli and—"

"Dev," he prompted.

"What?" she said, blinking.

His jaw tightened. "It's silly to insist on calling me Mr. Kohli when you've snuck into my yacht, into my bedroom, no less. Ridiculous to pretend that we don't know each other. On a level that strangers don't."

"That night has nothing to do with…today. Or now." At least her tone was steady even if her heartbeat wasn't.

He raised a perfect eyebrow. The man was more articulate with one gesture of his face than she was with all her words today, apparently. But then, it wasn't every day that Clare found herself riding a roller coaster of emotions, swinging from fear to betrayal to sheer lust.

"I'm having a hard time believing that."

Clare straightened, her hackles rising. "If you think I stowed away so that we could get…so that I can…" She could feel her face heating up again and cursed herself. "You've got this all wrong."

"Do I?"

"Yes. Absolutely. That night was a…one-off. I didn't hound your assistant for this meeting just so that I could wait for you in your bedroom. I'm not some sex-obsessed—"

"Then why are you here?" he hastily cut in.

"You need me," Clare said firmly. "That's why I'm here."

He stilled. "Excuse me?"

If she weren't stuck in a ridiculous predicament that threatened her very life, Clare would've found the outrage on his face hilarious. As if the world had turned upside down for him to need her.

"I need you?" he repeated, pushing his fingers through his hair.

Clare forged on, determined to keep his attention now that she had it. "What my company can do for you, I mean. This was supposed to be a business meeting tonight."

He shrugged. It caused all those delicious muscles in his chest to move in perfect harmony. The man shouldn't be allowed to wear his shirt open like that without a warning sign. "That's what I thought too," he said in a dry voice. Wary distrust was written all over his face. "Look, Clare. The last thing I need is to muddy the line between business and pleasure after what's happened to my company recently. I should've shut this meeting down the minute I realized we'd slept together."

She flinched.

"This—" he moved his hand between them, all masculine grace "—over."

And with that, he simply turned and walked away.

For a few seconds, Clare just stood there. She'd never been dismissed with such finality before. At least, not since she'd built The London Connection and made a name for herself in the world of PR.

After the cold indifference with which her aunt had welcomed her when her dad had dumped a five-year-old Clare on her unwilling doorstep like unwanted baggage, she'd made herself tougher. Grown a thick skin out of necessity. Day in, day out, she'd poured all that hurt and loneliness into getting good A-levels and then a business qualification. Into getting away from her aunt's long-suffering attitude.

And yet this stung.

Maybe because he was the one man Clare had ever let her guard down with.

Maybe because she wanted to see admiration and respect in those beautiful brown eyes of his, rather than contempt.

The last thing she wanted after her father had abandoned her was to run after another man who didn't care about her. Who thought she amounted to nothing.

The self-disgust turned to much-needed anger. That fresh burst of emotion propelled her forward before she realized what she was doing. Her hand landed on a warm, hard shoulder.

Clare pulled away abruptly, feeling as if she'd been electrocuted.

He turned, his frown morphing into a full-blown scowl.

Clare raised her palms and backed down. But not before the scent of warm, male skin invaded her nostrils and filled her with that strange longing once more. "Look, Dev," she said, ignoring his expression, "I know this looks bad, okay? But I had a reason for invading your privacy and hiding here. Stepping off the yacht tonight was literally the most dangerous thing I could have done. If you can give me just a few minutes, I'll explain everything."

"I'm not sure—"

"I took a chance on you. I went with my gut instinct instead of listening to what the rest of the world's saying about you right now. At the very least, you can afford me that same chance."

His jaw tight, he rubbed one long finger against his brow. As if he was at the end of his tether. "Explain yourself. About taking a chance on me," he said, as if it was the most outrageous thing he'd heard so far out of her mouth.

"I pitched for a meeting with you even though the entire world's gleefully painting you as a no-conscience, sexist monster who created a toxic work environment for women. Because I thought you should be given a chance to present your side too."

Despite the tension in his face, his mouth twitched at the corners. "So this is an altruistic effort on your part to save my backside?"

Clare shrugged. Trying very hard to not think of the backside in question. The very same one she'd so recently been dreaming of. "Not altruistic, no. I want my company to take over Athleta's PR on this side of the pond. I want a long, nicely padded contract that will put The London Connection on the map in North America. It will be a mutually beneficial arrangement."

A mutually pleasurable arrangement…that was what she'd said when she'd propositioned him that night.

The moment the words left her mouth, Clare knew she should literally have put it any other way. From the flare of awareness that lit up his eyes, he remembered it too.

After months of lusting over him from afar,

she'd finally made her move at the charity gala for Women Entrepreneurs. They'd crossed paths a few times at parties and conventions before that, but he'd always been with a different woman on his arm. Despite that, she'd heard about his reputation as a fair and kind man through the grapevine. On that night, Clare had won an award and had been feeling on top of the world. When she'd gone to get a drink, he'd been there. Offering congratulations with warm eyes and that mobile, laughing mouth. Taking her in.

"You don't know who I am, do you?" she'd asked laughingly. "Or what I've won the award for."

He'd dipped his head in acknowledgment. "No, sorry. They were giving out those awards faster than glasses of pink champagne."

She'd swatted his shoulder with her clutch. "Hey, mine was a shiny gold plaque, you know. The others were only silver."

"Well of course, that puts you a cut above the rest." The devilish charmer that he was, he'd batted those eyes at her. He had ridiculously long lashes and pretty eyes for a…well, for a man. Hand pressed to his chest, he'd mock bowed. "Not that the award isn't deserved. I've just had a long week and the details are a little fuzzy right now."

"Ahh…as long as you aren't seeing multiples of me," she'd quipped, shaking her head as the uniformed staff walked by with a tray of champagne. She'd already had bubbles in her belly and a pounding heart thanks to the man bending down to her from his impressive height.

Her belly had swooped even though his shoulder barely touched hers. He was so broad that he'd filled her entire view. His gaze held hers, front teeth digging into the way too lush lower lip of his. "Why do I have a feeling that it would be even more delightful to have multiples of you?"

Clare had blushed then. "How about you make it up to me for mocking my award?"

He'd finished his drink and turned to her. Shining the full blast of his attention on her. That gaze of his had turned perceptive and thoughtful. Less roguish and more…curious. Even admiring in a way that had sent tingles up and down her skin. "I don't remember your firm's name. But I did hear the emcee say you're a self-starter. A woman who forged her own path, despite an initial struggle. No one can take that away from you, can they?"

She'd been absolutely glowing by then. Inside and out. "No, they can't. As a self-starter yourself, you also know then that we have to milk every opportunity to the max. As I know who you are, but you don't have a clue about me, I have the upper hand between the two of us, right now."

"You're bloodthirsty," he said, leaning closer.

"Does that scare you?" she said, raising a brow, feeling a thrill she'd never known.

Another heart-stopping smile. "On the contrary, I have a weakness for a bloodthirsty woman who goes after what she wants."

"So?"

"So, your wish is my command, my lady," he'd said finally.

"Dance with me," she'd said boldly.

To her eternal delight, he'd taken her hand in his and led them to the dance floor. He'd asked her about the initiative that had garnered her the award. Her views on women in high positions and the obstacles they faced in a company's hierarchy.

With his arm warm and solid around her, his questions peppered with real interest, Clare had never felt so wanted. So…seen for herself.

A successful, moderately attractive woman who could hold her own with a brilliant, self-made entrepreneur. A man who could laugh at himself. A man who could admit he was wrong, apparently.

High on her success, determined to see if the attraction she felt was more than one-sided, Clare had wrapped her arms around his nape. And then she'd asked him directly, the words coming out of her mouth as if the torrent of desire couldn't be denied.

"Are you interested in taking this further?" She'd been so forthright, so honest.

His fingers had tightened on her waist, just a fraction. Sending an arrow of pleasure straight down to her belly. "How much further, exactly?"

"One whole night further."

There'd been a few long seconds where he'd just stared at her. Clare had felt as if she was standing on the cliff-edge of the entire world, ready to jump into the unknown with this man. "No strings?" he'd eventually said with a raised eyebrow.

"No strings," she'd confirmed with a bright smile.

And that had been it. No more words had been needed. At least not until he'd brought her to his suite and had asked her one tormenting question after the other about what she wanted. How she wanted it. When and where and how slow…or how fast or how deep…

Her wish had been his command, literally.

Clare didn't regret it for one moment. Not even now, when he was looking at her so suspiciously. He'd made their night together spectacular on more than one level—he'd been gentle and exploratory and funny…the perfect man. Just what Clare had needed.

Which was why she kept flinching at his nearness. It was a little hard to separate that perfectly wonderful man from this distrustful stranger who doubted her motives for being here.

But in spite of the wariness in his eyes, the knowledge of that night shimmered in the air around them. How hot and hard he'd been under her questing fingers. How he'd used those wickedly clever fingers to learn her rhythm. How deliciously heavy he'd felt over her when he'd ground his lean hips against hers.

A slow hum of heat built up under her skin but Clare ignored the feeling. Whatever had been between them was definitely over. This was all business now.

"Why are you so ready to help me?"

This she could answer with a certainty that had stayed with her despite how awkward things had become between them. "Because I saw how devastated you were when you looked at your phone that morning. How upset you were that something so awful had happened right under your nose." Even though she'd been hurt by his cold dismissal of her, she'd seen on his face the devastation the news had caused. That he was a man of integrity, just as she'd always known, made his ability to walk away from her so easily that much more...cutting.

When his gaze met hers, Clare rolled her eyes. "In the few moments before you threw me out of the hotel room, that is."

"I never threw you out. I said I was leaving."

"It was your suite," Clare said tartly, and then took a deep breath. "After I asked, in the most pathetic voice, if I had done something wrong." Heat flushed her neck and face, but Clare was determined to have it all out in the open. "You said it had been 'nice' but that's all it could be."

Dev rubbed a hand over his face, looking pained.

"The point is that…in those few minutes, before you replaced your mask of jaded billionaire playboy, I saw how genuinely shocked you were. I've followed the story as it exploded all over the media. The harm that was caused happened under your leadership. Everything you've said publicly since that interview, you've never once tried to get out of the fact that you'd failed your employee. Which made me believe that you should be given a chance to turn this around."

"And you're the one to do it?"

When it came to business, Clare never second-guessed herself. She'd built her company to be the best. "Your current PR firm sucks. I can do a much better job. The London Connection has a reputation of women empowerment initiatives. A good record of dragging draconic policies into the twenty-first century. Making companies equitable for all."

"How would this benefit you?" he asked, his gaze pinned on her face.

"Launched our North American branch with a bang? Built our reputation? Turned a big ship like Athleta around and made it a better place for women to work? Take your pick."

Irritation flickered in his gaze. "I don't need you to teach me how to fix this."

"No. I believe you've already implemented several measures."

"How would you know that?"

"Because, as I said, ever since that morning, I've kept an eye on you. You've hired an independent agency to comb through your HR. You've already promoted three different female executives into more senior positions. You've got an equality and diversity agency doing a private audit on your board of directors."

Again, one brow rose. Clare stared right back. She may have started this meeting on the wrong foot, but she'd never been second-rate when it came to her job.

"But you still need me to put a good spin on it. To make everyone, especially women, believe that Athleta will never make those mistakes again. In simple terms, I will validate your efforts. Isn't that why you finally agreed to see me, Dev?"

He leaned against one wall, his gaze thoughtful. "I'll give you points for thorough research."

Clare shrugged. "But you still don't trust me?"

He shook his head "It's not you in particular that I don't trust."

She waited patiently. If she landed this contract, it would be a huge win for The London Connection. Both for their bottom line and their reputation. Not to mention that, right now, she had nowhere else to go. Literally.

When he finally spoke, tight lines bracketed

his mouth. The shock and stress she'd seen in his face that morning three weeks ago hadn't left him yet. "The man who harassed and hounded Ms. Lane out of the company, I've known him for fifteen years. He mentored me when I started in this business. He was one of my first seed investors.

"I… I delegated so much of the everyday operations of the company to him and the team he brought in. Mostly corporate bigwigs. Which meant their power and reach in the company was—" a nerve vibrated in his temple "—far more extensive than it should have been. Unchecked, even. Because I was too focused on the next deal, the next product launch. If you'd asked me a month ago, I'd have staked my reputation on the fact that he'd never abuse his power like that with a woman—with anyone. *Never*… And yet he did. While he worked for me." A curse fell from his mouth, echoing around the cabin. Full of anger and disgust and something more. "Trust is very thin on the ground for me right now. No matter who it is. He…"

"He made you doubt your own judgment," Clare said gently, picking the thread up. Knowing exactly how he was feeling right then. "You're wondering if you can ever get it back…that trust in yourself. You're not sure where else you might have made a mistake. You're struggling to come to terms with why you didn't see it when it was right in front of your eyes."

"Do you have a degree in psychology too, Clare?" His gaze shone with reluctant admiration. And despite the frustration on his face, that hint of humor peeked through. "Or are you gleaning all this from my expression too?"

Clare laughed. Because it was easier to laugh it away before the pain set in. Before she was forced to consider at length what all this meant and how it shattered the very foundation of her life. "No, no degree in psychology. Just a lot of life experience. Believe me when I say I perfectly understand where you're coming from." She took a step forward, intent on making him understand. "I'll prove to you without a doubt that I didn't hide in your bedroom just so I could seduce you all over again. Like I already told you, I have reasons of the life-threatening kind for invading your privacy."

"Fine. I'll ask the captain to bring us back into port, and you can explain that rather bizarre statement to me. We'll—"

"Why take us back into port?" she demanded, her thoughts in a panic again.

He stilled. "I'm en route to Rio de Janeiro, and then heading on to my remote villa in the Caribbean. I'm sure the last thing you want is to be stranded there with me for several weeks."

"I absolutely do want to be stranded at some remote villa in the Caribbean with you," she contradicted him urgently. "In fact, right now, that sounds like a heaven-sent solution to all my problems."

He raised a brow, not so much wary as leery of her motives now. "So you're admitting that you wanted to be stranded with me?"

She sighed, knowing that she was doing a horrible job of this. "Not stranded with you in a romantic setting but more stranded on an island where Mob bosses and their cheerful thugs can't get to me. I heard you say during the party that you were going to be sailing around, or whatever the hell you call it, for the next couple of weeks or so. That's the reason I stowed away."

That distrustful look was back in his eyes again. Not that she could blame him. Frustration and that familiar resentment sat like a boulder on Clare's chest. She'd slogged for so many years, carefully building her life so that she didn't need anyone in it. With one move, her father had negated everything she'd achieved. She was going to sound like a certifiable loon for saying what she was about to say.

"Explain, now," Dev said, in a hard tone that did wonders for the quagmire of self-pity that was threatening to engulf her. "And no more beating about the bush. Give it to me straight."

"Straight, right. Here goes… I'd like you to kidnap me."

He rolled his eyes. "Now I know you've lost your mind."

"No, I haven't," Clare said with a laugh. It was the hysterical note in it, she was sure, that finally convinced him. "I'm the original damsel in distress, stuck in one of those ghastly fairy tales that I used to love. It's not really hoots and laughs when you have to depend on someone else to rescue you, you know?" she said, her words full of a bitterness she hadn't even known was festering inside her. "I need to hide out with you until I can figure out how I can avoid becoming the wife or mistress of some Mafia boss. So much for all the women's empowerment I've been a part of, eh?"

CHAPTER THREE

DEV STARED AT the glittering sheen of tears in Clare's eyes. Like a mirage in a desert, the wet shine disappeared as he moved closer to her, despite his resolve to treat her as nothing more than a business colleague. If not for the tightness around that lush mouth of hers, he'd have thought he'd imagined the gleam of tears. If not for the stark fear that was palpably radiating from her—that made him want to wrap her safely in his arms—he'd have called her crazy and thrown off his yacht, ocean or not.

But as wary as he was currently feeling about his ability to judge someone's character, Dev had a feeling she was telling the truth. Or at least the truth as she believed it to be.

He reached out his hand, then pulled it back.

This is not a good idea, Dev, the rational voice in his head said. The one that had tried so many times to curb his wild behavior. The one that was most in touch with his innermost feelings, so to speak.

But, as much as he'd grown a thick, impervious skin over the past almost two decades—thanks to his military school discipline—he wasn't quite the uncaring bastard the media had so recently accused him of being. Or that he sometimes wished he could be, whenever he found himself caring too deeply, about anything. Especially when he was confronted with a woman like Clare Roberts and all the unwanted feelings she evoked in him.

What they both needed was to take a step back and regroup after this strange meeting, in his closet of all places. "Why don't we move this discussion out of here?" When she shot him a wary glance, he said gently, "You look like you need a drink. I definitely do, after getting yelled at by my twin."

"Oh, you have a twin?"

The twinkle in her eyes had him nodding. "Yes. She's incredibly bossy and she's getting married in about a month. She's just warned me that she'll cut me off from any future nieces or nephews she may give me if I don't make it to her wedding. So the deadline to clean up my image just got even tighter."

"Because you don't want the cloud of this scandal to disturb the wedding atmosphere?"

"No, because I can't go if..." Dev checked himself. Big blue eyes watched him curiously. "Doesn't matter why. It's just important to change the narrative on my company before the wedding. If I want to make it, that is."

She nodded, lifting that stubborn chin of hers. "Then our plan needs to be aggressive too."

He still didn't know why she was here. "I'd also like to have this talk while I'm not still standing half-undressed in my own closet and you don't look as if someone's done a thorough job of… mussing you up," he said tightly. For all his numerous girlfriends, he hated the idea of mixing business with pleasure. Even though the pleasure had been in the past in this case. "I trust most of my staff, but there's no guarantee of anyone's loyalty if there's a nice price tag attached to a juicy story."

Her mouth fell open. "You think someone might tell the press that you've trapped me aboard your yacht with the intention of having your wicked way with me?"

She looked so delighted at the prospect that Dev felt his mouth twitching. "You sound like that's not a bad thing."

"Not a bad thing at all, if I was, in reality, a willing partner," she said dreamily, her gaze suddenly far-off.

"Is this one of your fantasies then, Ms. Roberts?" he said, trying and failing to sound serious.

Her gaze swept over his chest, naked longing shining in it. If he wasn't just as hungrily tracing every feature of her face, he'd have missed it. The woman had no idea how arousing her transparent desire for him was. He was both amused and a little annoyed by it.

No, mostly annoyed, he corrected himself.

Because, he was right in his initial estimate of her. It had been sheer madness—accepting her proposition that night. In his defense, she'd looked incredibly sexy and pretty and had been so earnestly direct that he'd found her utterly irresistible.

Clare Roberts—for all she tried to pretend to be a femme fatale—was very much an innocent from the top of her head to the soles of her pretty feet. The kind he usually avoided like the plague.

"Clare?" he said, and cleared his throat. Desire was a constant low thrum under his skin that he had to get used to—because it couldn't be indulged in again.

"What?" she said distractedly, still only half present.

"Maybe this isn't the time to act out one of your fantasies?" Dev suggested, suddenly realizing he was grinning. It was just too much fun to bandy words with her. More fun than he'd had in a long time. "However, you might want to check what my interest level is after we finish our business dealings though."

She drew herself up to her full five feet three inches, glaring daggers at him. "You really think

I'm standing here daydreaming about being kidnapped by you, don't you?"

He shrugged, laughing. "Well, there's nothing wrong with kidnapping when we're both consenting adults, is there? And who am I to stand in the way of a woman's sexual fantasy? Thirdly, you're the one who got all dreamy and soft when I mentioned it."

"I was considering it as a story that could be carefully directed so that it reached the right ears, yes. Not getting all hot and bothered about you having your wicked way with me," she denied hotly.

"That's me put in my place then," he said, with a sigh. "As for a story about you and me being stuck together, Clare, forget it. The last thing I need is any unwelcome scrutiny on my love life."

"But what if it serves my purpose?"

"It doesn't serve mine," Dev growled, realizing she was serious. What the hell was she talking about now? "Do you want this deal with my company or do you want salacious stories about us in the media?"

"I want both."

Dev frowned. Maybe he had been too quick to trust this woman. "I think you'd better tell me the reason you're here first," he said. "Everything else can come later."

He saw her take a deep breath.

"I have a Mob boss after me. His hired thug

was here, aboard your yacht this evening, watching me. It was why I had to play hide-and-seek in your closet."

"What?" Dev said, incapable of any other response. He arrested the stinging denial that rose to his lips. The stark fear in her eyes couldn't be a lie.

"The same man was camped outside my office in London. Then I saw him when I flew to a conference in New York. Then again here. When I spotted him up there tonight," she said, pointing to the upper deck, her entire body shivering at some invisible draft, "I just had to hide. I'm sorry for thrusting this all on you, especially when you have your own problems, but I had no choice. I'm stuck in a really bad situation."

"I know the man you're referring to. I signaled to my head of security after I saw him approach you. He was definitely not on the guest list. When I checked again, he'd disappeared."

Clare simply nodded. "I had a call from his boss as I arrived here tonight. He told me that he was going to have me, no matter what. That no one's going to stop him, because he owns me outright."

Dev saw her shiver again and fisted his hands. "You're safe here. My security escorted his henchman off the yacht."

"I'm safe for now," she corrected.

"Why is he after you?"

Her lashes fell down in a curtain, suddenly hiding her expression. "I took money from a man I shouldn't have trusted."

Dev couldn't help sounding incredulous. "You took a loan from a known Mob boss? Why?"

Pink scoured her cheeks. "I told you it was…a bad decision. I was desperate to establish my business. I didn't look closely at who I was trusting."

Dev raised a brow. "So wait, you took out a loan with yourself as collateral? How can a woman specializing in PR not understand what she was signing?"

"Please don't use it as a measure of my efficiency. Let's just say I found myself tricked. Those weren't the terms that were spelled out when I accepted the money. I was just so happy to have a running start on establishing my business. I…" She rubbed her temple with her fingers, her gaze anywhere but on him. "It doesn't matter why or how this happened, okay? That damned man thinks he owns me now."

Clare Roberts was a perplexing combination of innocence and sophistication, with a good measure of idiocy thrown in. Or had she been that desperate to launch her business? To establish her self-sufficiency? To prove her own self-worth?

Because those feelings of desperation were very old friends to Dev.

"I just need some time to figure a way to get

out of his clutches. Somewhere he and his goons can't reach me. The last thing I want is to become the prized possession of some Mafia boss who'll delight in punishing me by lending me to his lieutenants whenever he feels like it."

"And how would you know he'd do that?" Dev asked, his mouth twitching again.

She looked at him and away, embarrassment shining in her face. "I binge-watched a show where the main character did that. Fairy tales and fantasies are not really what you'd associate with a practical businesswoman like me, are they?" A bitterness he knew only too well twisted her mouth.

"We all have our guilty pleasures, Clare."

"Like you and your never-ending array of bed partners?" she retorted. But before he could answer her, she shook her head regretfully. "Let's pretend I didn't just say that. And no, I don't need rescuing by anyone. I just need time to rescue myself. So?"

"So what?" he said, wondering what he was signing up for here.

"Will you let me stay aboard for a little while?"

Dev studied her. With her mussed-up hair and clothes, she couldn't have looked less like the CEO of her own PR firm. She looked like trouble. Of the kind that he didn't usually touch with a very long pole.

The last thing he needed right now was another headache. And yet, he couldn't just throw her out, could he? Not when he'd seen the very man she'd mentioned eyeing her like a particularly juicy steak. Not when stark fear at her plight had rendered her so distressingly pale.

He'd already let down one woman who'd been under his protection. Had failed in what he considered to be one of the most important aspects of his own personality—defending those who couldn't defend themselves.

Those who were deemed lesser or weaker, just because they didn't fit a certain definition of perfect or normal. He had been that kid once, with no champion to defend him. With no one to understand how he'd felt being cut off from the world of the written word. Especially not after Mama's death.

How could he ignore Clare's plight now, knowing that her life might be in danger? He didn't want any more women on his conscience.

He looked down to find her gaze resolutely staring back at him. "All I'm asking for is a place to hide. Whether you hire me or not to clean up your image, you can decide that based on my proposal."

More than pleasantly surprised at how fast she'd turned all that emotion into something far more constructive, he impulsively said, "Fine. We'll figure out a way to get you out of this predicament."

He wondered who was more shocked by his ridiculous promise. Playing the hero had never been his forte. Emotional grandstanding of the kind that his father excelled in had always made him wary. So why was he spouting these words to her?

Thankfully, Clare apparently had a lot more sense and gumption than he had given her credit for.

She shook her head. "Now, Mr. Kohli, don't go making promises you can't keep. Even when I buried myself in fairy tales and stories, I knew enough to not think myself the heroine. To not lose my grip on reality." She sounded like a woman who had never had anyone to depend on. She sounded exactly like him. Dev wondered if that was her appeal for him. "This is a problem I'll solve for myself. As I've always done. All I ask is that you buy me some time."

"Are we really back to being Mr. Kohli and Ms. Roberts again then?"

"I think it's safest, don't you? Especially now that you might be one of my biggest clients."

Dev grinned. There was something about the sudden, starchy formality that she was insisting on that made him want to unravel her. Just a little bit. "Afraid you might not be able to resist me while we're stuck together, are you?"

She laughed. "You think this is being stuck together?" Her arms moved around to encompass the vast yacht. "Aboard your gigantic yacht. It's so ridiculously huge that one might be tempted to think the owner was overcompensating for something…"

Dev took a step forward. One step. There was still a lot of distance between them for him to reach her. Her mouth clamped shut. "You're being unfair, Ms. Roberts."

"How?"

"Making wildly absurd claims that I can't rebut without making statements that could be construed as innuendo? You're baiting me, knowing that I can't play along. You're having your own sweet little revenge."

She blushed and looked away, and he smiled in satisfaction.

"As long as we're clear on the fact that this is not some kind of invitation to re—"

"Yes, yes, I know it's not." She cut in, rolling her eyes. "I'm not stupid. Also, I'm not into skittish playboys who have to be convinced what a treasure I am."

"Did you just call me skittish?" Dev let out an outraged growl and now it was her mouth that twitched.

Her blue eyes widened as she considered him. "I'm not going to crimp your style by being here, am I?"

"What do you mean?" he demanded, feeling surly. Because there was that hum of desire under his skin again. Suddenly the idea of being stuck with this woman for however long—without being able to kiss that lovely mouth—was nothing but pure torment.

"Do you have anyone else on board, Mr. Kohli?"

"Other than my staff, no," he said, wondering where she was going with this.

"A girlfriend? An ex? A bunch of guests waiting to participate in an orgy?"

He pursed his lips. "No."

"Good, then I don't have to disillusion some poor girl looking for a good time?"

"Is that comment in general or specific, Ms. Roberts?"

"Both. We have to be really careful about who you choose as your next playmate."

"Ah…so you were bothered by my behavior that morning then?" He had no idea why he was pressing the issue. No idea why this particular woman had been so stubbornly stuck in his thoughts for weeks.

To give her credit, Clare didn't look away this time. Dev thought she was incredibly brave because her eyes shimmered with a truth she didn't give voice to.

He knew he had hurt her that morning. But it wasn't something he could change or even regret. Better she understood the truth about him now rather than build any ridiculous expectations of this…partnership.

It had to be strictly business.

"That's because I wasn't used to the morning after protocol," she said, all dignified effrontery. The twist of her mouth was both a challenge and something more…something that made Dev want to taste and absorb into himself. "And it was quite a hard landing after the ride you took me on that night. A girl should be forgiven for floating about on an endorphin rush. She needs a little time to recover from seducing you."

Dev burst out laughing. "For the sake of honesty, you didn't seduce me. I seduced you."

Clare was shaking her head and advancing on him suddenly. "No way. I had a plan, and I implemented it to perfection." When his eyes twinkled with a wicked mirth, she stopped.

Dev had no idea how she continually opened doors he didn't want to see through. But she did. "Of course, you had a plan." He shook his head, laughing. Remembering how she'd taken the chance he'd given her. How she'd neatly cornered him into a fascinating conversation and then a whole lot more.

"Why do anything without doing it well?"

He met her gaze again. But Clare looked away, as if that one moment of honesty had been indulgent enough. Reality intruded on them, bursting the bubble of awareness.

Clare knew she should be glad. But there was something about this man that made her not only feel hot and bothered but also naive and foolish. "Anyway, that night's done with. We need to move on from it."

But even now, as she studied his hard jaw, there was a part of her—that foolish part again—that wished he'd tell her that despite what he'd said to her that morning, he'd actually wanted to take her in his arms again. That he'd wanted to see her again afterward.

"Do I have your word that this won't become awkward between us?" he asked, interrupting her reverie with a nice heaping dose of reality.

"Of course you do," she said with extra vehemence. "I told you the reason I snuck in here. And now we've cleared that up, I can absolutely assure you I have no romantic notions whatsoever about you, Mr. Kohli. However, not hiring my company to clean up your image just because we slept together is its own kind of…"

His frown turned into a ferocious scowl. "What?"

"Unfairness," she said, amending her words. "Our sexual history shouldn't affect my career, Mr. Kohli. I shouldn't be penalized for going to bed with you."

"I agree with that a hundred percent," he said, releasing a sigh. He clasped his jaw in his palm, tension radiating from his frame. And then he looked at her. Clare braced herself. "You'll have to forgive me if I'm being extra distrustful of everyone right now," he said honestly, taking the wind from her sails yet again.

"I understand."

They eyed each other carefully—not exactly adversaries, but not friends either. But… Clare couldn't help thinking there was also a certain level of trust between them, even though he'd tried to be all cold and calculating about his decision to work with her. How could there not be a certain warmth between them when they'd been as intimate as they had? When whatever had pulled them together was still tangibly in the air, crackling into life every time they were within touching distance?

She might not have a whole lot of experience with men. But she knew what desire looked like on this particular man's face. She knew him a lot better than he thought, or she liked.

"I promise you that you won't regret taking me on, Mr. Kohli. I'll have my proposal ready for you by first thing tomorrow morning."

Dev shook his head. "Let's make it a bit later in the day. I have a lot of things to get through tomorrow. Why don't you at least take the morning off?"

"And do what?" She looked so dumbstruck by the suggestion that Dev laughed.

"Just lounge about. Recover from the stress of

fleeing that man. Take a bath. Catch up on sleep. We'll meet later tomorrow afternoon some time when I'm free."

She nodded. But he knew it was a reluctant acquiescence. "Okay."

Dev stepped aside to let her pass. When she reached the doorway, he called her name, feeling a strange tightness in his chest.

"Yes, Mr. Kohli?" she said, her gaze steady.

"If you want my help getting out of this predicament you've landed yourself in, I'll need the entire truth from you."

And just as Dev had expected, she colored immediately, confirming his suspicions. He knew there had been something wrong with her story.

Her gaze turned stubborn. "There's nothing more to say. I trusted a man I shouldn't have. I…let my heart rule my head and made a stupid decision. I'm willing to help you clean up your mess. All I ask is that you give me a little time to clean up mine."

Dev had never met a woman who could turn the tables on him so well. And she was right. He knew firsthand the price of letting one's guard down. The price of fighting your battles alone. "Fine. We're partners, Ms. Roberts."

"Perfect, Mr. Kohli. You'll see you're right to trust me in this."

With that parting shot, she walked out of his cabin. Confirming his second suspicion that

Clare Roberts was anything but the uncomplicated woman he'd thought her to be when he'd taken her to his bed.

CHAPTER FOUR

DURING THE TIME until their meeting—which to Clare felt like an eternity, since she'd been working without a break ever since she'd graduated from university—she explored Dev's gigantic superyacht. She couldn't help but be impressed, even though she'd teased him about the sheer size of it.

Even if she hadn't already known it after their night together, the more she researched his company, and the man himself, the more Clare learned that Dev Kohli didn't have any need whatsoever to prove his masculinity to anyone. So his yacht, other than being a supreme symbol of his success and stamina, was definitely not just a possession to be strutted in front of the world.

In a perverse way, it would have been so much easier to deal with the man if he'd neatly fitted into a preconceived mold.

Playboy—only cares about bedding women, not keeping them safe from evil henchmen.

Billionaire—cares about nothing except making his next billion.

Playboy billionaire—balding, beer-bellied old man with no humor lurking in his brilliant brown eyes.

But it seemed the man was a trendsetter in this too.

Following his advice, Clare had indulged herself last night with a long soak in the huge tub in her cabin's en suite bathroom, consciously reminding herself that she was safe. For now. At least from external events and Mafia villains. Physically, she was safe.

Emotionally…well, she'd survived for years on indifference, using her big dreams to propel her forward. And that's what she was going to do now too—turn this calamity into an opportunity and move forward with nothing but sheer determination.

Simply because there was no other choice except survival. If she had to be on the run, she'd prefer it to be on the luxury yacht of a man she trusted.

Snuggled in a thick robe that dragged on the lush carpet under her feet, she'd arrived in her bedroom to find hot soup and warm, crusty tomato and cheese sandwiches. Luckily, no one had been around to hear the loud growl her stomach had emitted. She'd tucked herself into another window seat that offered a gorgeous nighttime view of the blue ocean and finished her bedtime snack in a matter of seconds.

Digitally blacked out windows and cool, dark navy-blue furnishings had helped her fall asleep in minutes, all thoughts of kidnapping villains dissolving like mist.

When she'd jerked awake the next morning, warm in the nest of soft bedclothes, Clare realized she'd slept for ten hours straight—a miracle in itself. Not counting how normal and in control she felt after another quick shower.

Clearheaded and alert for the first time in days, she wished she'd done her hiding in a different bedroom and not faced Dev yesterday, when she'd been afraid for her life. She'd made a right little numpty of herself.

She hadn't built The London Connection by acting like a witless fool or a dreamy-eyed twit. The future of her company was even more paramount now than it had been before. Since, thanks to her father, she apparently owed a huge amount of money to a mobster. There was no margin for messing this up with Dev. She needed to keep her focus on it being all business between them, as he'd said.

Ten hours of sleep did wonders for a girl. The stern talking-to she gave herself as she blow-dried her hair boosted her confidence. She made do with the lip-gloss, concealer and mascara in her handbag.

Having enveloped herself in another thick towel, she spent the next twenty minutes, looking through the large but mostly vacant closet attached to her cabin. Luckily, she, Amy, Bea all made it a policy to carry spare underwear and all kinds of paraphernalia in their bags for any PR emergency. But she had no clothes.

As she eyed the almost empty wardrobe, she thought of her travel bag sitting in her hotel room in São Paulo, now all but lost. There was no way she could have sneaked it past security onto the yacht last night. For a few seconds, she indulged in the idea of wearing last night's skirt and blouse again. But then she remembered that before she'd got into that lovely warm bath, she'd dropped them into the conveniently placed laundry basket, which was now, of course, empty.

Apparently, the man's yacht ran as efficiently as his sportswear empire.

In the end, Clare ripped the packaging off one of Dev's dress shirts. Apparently, the man had designer dress shirts lying around in all the cabins. Savile Row deserved better, but she didn't care right then. Thinking for too long on why she was here on a stranger's yacht, sailing away to some idyllic island with her company's fate and her own hanging in the balance might lead to falling into the pit of despair and fury she was somehow keeping at bay.

With the shirt hanging almost to her knees,

Clare used a belt and turned it into a dress. Back on went her leather stilettos, and she looked halfway decent. Or at least that's what she told herself.

After getting lost in a service elevator and ending up in a theater room, and discovering a neatly stowed away seaplane on the top deck, it began to dawn on Clare that the yacht was also the man's home. And that while he had invited her to explore, it had been mostly a polite response to a distressed and wild-tale-weaving woman he'd found in his closet. Not the welcome mat precisely.

With each space she invaded, it became clearer that he was a man who absolutely protected his privacy at all costs. Because for all the features in the media detailing his jet-setting life and fast girlfriends, no journalist had ever been allowed access to this yacht.

This was where Dev Kohli, former gold-medal-winning swimmer and billionaire playboy, retreated to when the alternately adoring and punishing world's media became all too much.

Like the man himself, while the exterior was all gleaming confidence, the interior had depths she couldn't plumb in a year, much less a day. There was none of the gold accents and veneer, or the traditional nautical motifs she'd imagined from peeking at antiquated travel magazines her dentist had lying around the office.

Up and down, Clare went, fascinated by it all. After getting lost again, she armed herself with a schematic map and a picnic basket from the galley—apparently, they had been given express instructions to look after Mr. Kohli's guest properly—and shamelessly explored the yacht.

Admiring this example of twenty-first-century engineering was definitely better than pondering one's fate as an owned woman. Or even worse, daydreaming about a man's happy trail. In the end, Clare settled into a lounger on the main deck, her picnic basket by her side, her laptop on her knee. The noonday sun glinted off the water in brilliant golden sparkles, while colorful coastal towns were visible in the distance.

If a man was disposed to moving from place to place, disinclined to put roots down…then clearly, Dev Kohli did it in style.

But, she mused, if all this wealth was at her disposal, the last place she'd want to be was on the sea. There was a temporariness to moving from place to place that didn't appeal to Clare. Even having been disillusioned again and again by her dad's unending lies over the years, that he would come for her and that they would be a family again, and by her aunt's indifference toward her, Clare had always wanted a permanent home.

A grand home and an even grander family of noisy sisters and brothers and nieces and nephews, celebrating birthdays and festivals together, prying into each other's business and making up after silly fights and all that sort of thing.

But with each year rolling around and her dad not showing up, it had become increasingly distant. Then he'd given her the money she'd used to start up her business, just before he died. She'd thought he would have been proud to know she'd used the money so well, but even that daydream had turned sour. Because the man her father had borrowed that money from had finally discovered her father was dead and couldn't pay it back, and so he'd come after Clare.

She was truly alone in the world and couldn't escape the knowledge that to put her in such danger, her father had never really cared for her at all.

She still couldn't wrap her head around that bit of news. Couldn't get her jumbled feelings to make any kind of sense. They just sat in the pit of her stomach like a knotted lump. For years, a foolish part of her had believed that he'd somehow turn into an ideal father one day. When he'd sent her the money, she'd thought her faith in him had finally been validated. That he had loved her in his own way.

But once again, she'd lied to herself.

Her laptop screen blurred in front of her eyes and Clare blinked hard.

No, she couldn't let the past muddle her future. Her vision cleared when she saw a social media photo turn up in her search results. She stared at the tall, gorgeous brunette—a model, of course, who had just revealed her...association with Dev. Clare's mind instantly did a quick calculation of whether she herself had come before or after this model, in his life.

The very idea of being just another night of transient pleasure to him grated on her nerves. But that was who he was. Dev Kohli was clearly allergic to relationships that lasted longer than a couple of weeks—if that.

She'd do well to remember that simple fact.

Pursing her lips, Clare added a bullet point to the list of things she needed to discuss with him.

It was going to take all the finesse she possessed to make sure Dev understood what he needed to do. So Clare once again pushed away the sorrow and grief that was crouching inside her chest and instead poured her energy into outlining the proposal for saving Athleta.

Focusing on her business, on tangible targets and not naive dreams, had always been her lifeline.

Clare blinked and opened her eyes as a short man in a pristine black-and-white uniform informed her that Mr. Kohli was waiting to see her now in his study. She sat up and straightened her shirt, aghast at the fact that she'd fallen asleep again after only a few hours' work. God, what sort of strange inertia and exhaustion had her in its grip?

Before the uniformed man disappeared to wherever it was that people seemed to hide on the monstrous yacht, she begged him to point her in the direction of the study.

Even with his instructions, it took her ages to find her way to there. It seemed the very universe was constantly conspiring to make her look un-professional in front of the one man she wanted to impress with her smarts and sophistication and efficiency.

Laptop and a folder in hand, Clare walked into an expansive circular room with a dizzyingly high ceiling. Light filtered through the skylight in the center of it, casting a golden glow over the floor-to-ceiling shelves of books. Rows and rows of books were filed with almost military preci-sion. Clare let out a soft sigh, the idea of spending hours and hours lost in the library in this study would be pure heaven to her.

The sound of a throat clearing jerked her at-tention away from the world of rare first editions.

In a sunken seating area, in the midst of the airy space, was Dev. Looking for all intents and purposes like a king sitting amid his priceless treasures. Except his treasures, it seemed, were books. Clare instantly knew that this space was different from everywhere else on the yacht. That this room somehow reflected his true nature. That if she wanted to know more about Dev Kohli—

the real man beneath the billionaire playboy persona—this was where she would find him.

Not that it was something she did want, she told herself.

Still, she felt a totally unnecessary and unbidden spark of excitement at being given a view of his inner sanctum that he hadn't allowed anyone else.

Dressed in black trousers and a white dress shirt that was unbuttoned at his throat, he looked elegant and masculine and somehow edgy at the same time. His carefully cut hair was rumpled and not quite perfect today. He reminded Clare of a restless predator she'd once seen on a documentary. As if there was a constant hum of energy beneath that sleek brown skin and taut muscles. As if at any moment, he might leap up from the beige leather sofa and launch himself into...

"Ms. Roberts?"

The deep timbre of his voice made Clare start. "Yes, Mr. Kohli?" she replied tartly, irritated with her own woolgathering. Neither did she miss the affected formality in the way he said her name.

"I asked if you were unwell." His gaze swept over her face and body. Had been doing so for a while, she realized. From her hair to the shirt—his shirt that she'd styled into a dress—to the belt and stilettos, he took in every little detail about her. She felt the quick scrutiny like a warm caress, pooling in places she didn't want to think about right now. "We can do this another time if you're still feeling the effects of—"

"Of course not. I'm perfectly fine. Thank you for asking." Her response sounded chillingly polite to her own ears. A bit too chilly, in contrast to the laid-back humor she saw in his eyes.

Suddenly, she had a feeling that he'd caught her napping on the main deck. Her chin lolling against her chest, with drool pooling at the side of her mouth, most probably.

"I've been ready for this meeting for a while." She sighed. "Only I had no idea how to reach you or any other human on this boat. "Did you get a chance to look at the initial contracts I emailed you?"

"No, it will take me to time to get to them. And it's a yacht, not a boat."

"On this oversized yacht," she parroted obediently, something under her skin humming awake at the twitch of that gorgeous mouth. The man often seemed to be on the verge of laughing. At the world, instead of with it, she suspected. And then of course, that thought led her to unwisely mutter, "Are you laughing at me, Mr. Kohli?"

He shook his head, but the mirth in his eyes remained. "Should I find something funny about this?"

"No. That's what I meant to point out. Nothing about this predicament is funny and yet—"

"Of course it's not. But you have to afford me

some allowances when you turn up here, your nose high in the air, determined to find something or other about me to disapprove of."

"That's not at all what I was thinking," she hotly denied.

"Then tell me what is it that you don't like about my yacht," he asked, surprising her yet again.

"What's there to not like?" she retorted, trying to keep her tone steady. Dev was so dangerous in how easily he could read her thoughts. "Like I said, it's big and beautiful."

"And yet, you just called it oversized, implying it's ostentatious."

"That was uncalled for," she said, forcing regret into her voice. Why did the man care so much what she thought of his damned yacht?

"I sense that you don't usually make uncalled-for statements, Ms. Roberts. Or that you say anything at all unless you mean it."

Their gazes held, his probing and lazily amused and hers...resisting the pull of his. It seems she was always resisting something or other about this man. Except the one time she'd stopped resisting and given in to desire, it had been glorious. She desperately hoped she wasn't wearing the jumble of her thoughts openly on her face.

"You're right, of course," she said, acquiescing. *Pick your battles, Clare*, came something that sounded very much like Bea's voice in her head. "It just seems like a lot of room for only one man."

"Ahh…you're going to lecture me about the environment and such? In my meager defense, I do travel with two personal assistants, three lawyers, a personal trainer and stylist, two chefs and a variety of other personnel—"

"Who I'm sure all contribute toward the larger-than-life image of you that mere mortal men can only aspire to."

"There it is again, Ms. Roberts." He raised an eyebrow. "That faint whiff of disapproval."

"Even though I've had a glimpse into the jet-setting lifestyles of certain celebrities while I've been working, I still find myself in awe of how much social media conceals from our eyes. How one-dimensional we want our celebrities to be. Nothing personal, Mr. Kohli."

His brows drew close as he regarded her thoughtfully, no quick response forming on that gorgeous mouth. That she had surprised him was clear by the sudden silence. But the buzz under her skin that was still there regardless of what he said or did…she so badly wished she could completely smother that involuntary reaction to him.

"You sound disappointed in me." He sounded comically confused. As if it was impossible for any woman to not delight in him!

"Something like that," she said, thankful that he was so far off the mark. It wouldn't do to cater to his giant ego. She had to keep this attraction purely inside her own head. "So you have a veritable army of servants," she said, refusing to let him unsettle her with that silent scrutiny, "who are of course paid to be neither seen nor heard. I can be forgiven, I think, for imagining us to be practically alone on board."

He ran a hand through his hair, looking slightly uncomfortable.

She scrunched her nose. "I wasn't actually intending to lecture you, you know."

"No?"

"I read the interview you did a while ago for that lifestyle magazine. You run a billion-dollar empire that has offices in five different countries. You have eleven thousand three hundred and seventy-six employees around the world. Not counting the personnel you employ here on the yacht and across the two flats, three estates and one palace you have dotted around. What was it that you said…you've created *an economy all on its own*? So all of this luxury is simply a place to rest for a man who gives livelihoods to so many. You called it your kingdom. And you said your mother taught you that a king has both duties and privileges. That was a nice personal touch," she added dryly.

"What, that I have duties and privileges?"

"No, mentioning your mother."

A hardness entered his eyes that transformed

his face from having an easy charm to a powerful remoteness. "It wasn't scripted to manipulate my audience, Ms. Roberts." His voice could cut through ice.

Clare nodded pacifyingly. Clearly, his family was a sore topic of conversation. She braced herself for the battle ahead. He wasn't going to like her plan one bit if he was ruffled at the mention of an old interview in which he'd referenced his mother.

"I never said there wasn't any truth to your interview." She eyed him as he sprawled on the circular leather sofa, surveying her with those long-lashed eyes. "You certainly do live like a king, Mr. Kohli."

One arm stretched along the sofa. The folded cuffs of his white shirt displayed a smattering of faint hair over strong forearms. Everything about the man was clean lines and masculine elegance. "You remember a lot about that interview."

Clare tried to not bristle at the inherent teasing in his tone. "I've always had a good memory for details. And it was clear that journalist came to you with an agenda."

"What do you think that might have been?"

"To lump you in with the current crop of spoiled, rich billionaires who don't give a damn about the state of the world. And you disarmed her very easily."

Far too easily, if you asked her. There was a

unique quality about Dev—and she didn't just mean his astonishingly good looks—that put women at ease with him. But an inherently welcoming sense of safety and fairness he extended, probably without knowing it himself.

Of course, he wasn't a saint by any means. He rarely dated anyone more than a few times, but Clare didn't blame any woman for succumbing to the fantasy of being this man's lover. Of hoping that she might be the only woman he wanted in his bed, the only woman he allowed into his life. And heart.

Which was definitely a fantasy, all right. But she…she was made of sterner stuff. More importantly, she'd already had her one fantasy night with him, which was apparently all he was going to deign to allow her.

"So what is it in particular that you don't like about the yacht? Or was it just me who riled you up when you walked in just now?"

"I just…fine, yes, it's a lovely yacht. Airy and light—and don't think I haven't noticed in the information brochures about how it's built with recycled wood and other environmentally friendly materials. But it seems so empty."

"Empty?" he said, his gaze shifting to encompass the furniture around them.

"It's just a personal thing."

His elbows dropping to his thighs, he leaned forward invitingly. "Tell me."

"All this wealth on open display…it seems counterintuitive to what we're all supposed to be pursuing, isn't it?"

He frowned. "And what is that?"

"Happiness. Peace. A place to belong."

"And you think that's what we're all looking for?" He didn't sound quite put off by her opinion, but it was clear that he didn't like it much either.

"You did insist on hearing my explanation, Mr. Kohli," she said pointedly. "I just meant that it feels somewhat isolated. Designed to be cut off from the world. The home of a man who doesn't want to put down any roots."

A bleakness entered his eyes then, and Clare was sure she'd crossed some imaginary boundary she shouldn't have. Trespassed where she wasn't invited, much less wanted.

"Ahh…then it's a good thing that you don't know me quite as well as you think you do," he said, that momentary vulnerability disappearing with a slow, lazy blink.

"I quite disagree," she added, something inside her pushing her on. "The thing is, I've spent quite a few hours recently deep diving into your life, and what's in the media does paint quite a cold, clinical picture of you. Flashy affairs that end faster than people change their car tires and business deal upon business deal where you always emerge the winner. In fact, you appear to lead what looks to the outsider like a very…solitary, selfish kind of life."

"So you're telling me you don't approve of my lifestyle?"

"Not at all," Clare retorted. "I admit that I do try to avoid men who tend to forge their own path and leave people behind along the way, yes, but this isn't about me. There's a world of difference between what you've allowed the world to see and what you're really like beneath all that shine and glamor."

"Despite your…deep dive—" his distaste for the term couldn't be clearer and his nostrils flared with a rare show of temper "—into my life, you still don't really know me. I'm not interested in pursuing all those things you mentioned. Why tie yourself to one place when instead you can have the freedom to explore the entire world?" He moved his hand between them dismissively, as if the things she mentioned were totally unimportant. "Belonging anywhere is overrated, Ms. Roberts. The only time the world listens to you is when you dictate to it. On your own terms."

He was drawing clear boundaries, and it would be wise for her to follow them. And yet she couldn't help feeling this impression he was giving right now, of a man who wanted to conquer the entire world, was just a mask he was putting on.

A facade he had to display in public.

But whether her suspicions were true or not, it wasn't her business, Clare reminded herself. The man was telling her who and what he was, and she should stop searching for qualities in him that weren't present. She'd done this with her dad too. Year after year, she'd convinced herself that he would come back for her one day. When the truth was, he'd barely even bothered ringing her on her birthday or at Christmas.

Clare gave her assent with a nod. "Fine, Mr. Kohli. As you say."

"Toeing the line now, Clare?"

She shrugged. "It's not my job to moralize to you, is it? It's to make you look perfect in front of the world. To give this shiny veneer of yours a human element. And for the most part, I'm glad to have followed my instinct about you."

"Which instinct is that?"

Clare lost her patience. "That you aren't the villain the world is calling you, Mr. Kohli," she said sweetly.

He grinned. "So how are you going to improve my image? And for heaven's sake, please can you stop calling me Mr. Kohli in that prissy voice?"

"Fine. Your love life…it's a trail of broken hearts and short affairs that don't paint a homely picture of you."

"I didn't realize we were trying to find me a bride."

Clare rolled her eyes. "This isn't funny, Dev.

For example, did you know that <u>one</u> of your exes, Sahara Jones, has taken to posting old pics of you and her on her social media this past week? Apparently, your breakup three months ago didn't suit her. She's got seven and a half million rabid followers who're all dying to know if you're back together as she's been hinting at and who'll turn into an angry mob at just one word from her. Is Ms. Jones going to brew more trouble for you in the coming weeks?"

"What do you mean?" he asked, surprisingly slow for a man who'd cut such a swathe through the worlds of competitive sport and then business with a dangerously irresistible combination of charm and smarts.

"Is she the type to drag your name through the mud? Plaster private information about you all over social media and make you look horrible? Because, right now, your reputation can't take any more hits."

"Of course not."

"And yet I'll point out that she was here on board your yacht last night—I recognized her. Presumably she was there without your knowledge?"

"You miss nothing," he said, jaw tight. Grudgingly.

"I don't. Neither did I miss that you had her escorted out by security with very little ceremony and that she didn't look very happy about it. So details, please."

"Excuse me?"

"I need details of your breakup so that I can gauge the possible consequences for myself."

His muttered something under his breath. "Sahara and I dated for just over two weeks. I ended our relationship, such as it was, when I realized she had no intention of respecting my privacy.

"On our second date, she sprung some talk show host on me so that we could both discuss all the disadvantages we'd each had to overcome to succeed. She was in talks with her agent about writing a book about our relationship. As you know, she's a model, but not massively famous and she had to jump through a lot of hoops to get there."

"And?" Clare prompted.

"She thought she'd ride the wave to stardom with me as her golden ticket. But I wasn't interested in a woman who was trying to probe into aspects of my life that were none of her business."

"What kind of salacious details did she manage to uncover?"

His jaw tightened. "There were no salacious details, Clare. She had no business thinking she could sell my life story as some romantic journey we were on together. I told my lawyers to sue her if she so much as whispers anything about me again. After the show she put on last time, she was fired from her latest contract. She was here last night to convince me that it had never been her idea in the first place. To help her land a different contract."

"Are you going to help her?"

Dev rubbed a hand over his face and sighed. "Yes. I'm not a callous bastard, Clare. I've already put her in touch with a friend of mine. Even though Sahara should've known better than to drag me into her drama."

"So I should count the matter as being resolved for now?"

"Yes."

"Why?"

"How do I know she won't create more trouble?" The frost in his eyes sent a small shiver down her spine. "Because she got what she wanted from me."

Clare nodded, biting back the question that lingered on her lips. "Can I suggest then, Dev, that until we make sure the world is firmly on your side, that you give up...women?"

The dratted man laughed. A full-bodied, rollicking kind of laugh that made her breath hitch in her throat. That transformed his face from a collection of perfectly symmetrical features to something altogether beautiful. A dimple sliced the hollow of his cheek and his eyes shone. "I don't think I've ever been ordered around quite so strictly in my life."

"Not even by your mother?" Clare added, enjoying the beauty of his smile and the warm fuzzies it aroused in her belly far too much.

He sobered instantly, but the warmth in his eyes lingered. "No. Not even by Mama. Not even when I made her life hell. Not even when I frustrated her no end and caused her grief." He gave a sigh that seemed to rock through the solid core of him. "My mother was one of those souls that was all love and patience and kindness itself."

"The point is," Clare said, wanting to chase away the shadows that crossed his face at the mention of his lovely sounding mother, "that when it comes down to it, hiring me to clean up your image is exactly like being in school with a very strict headmistress. This might never work if you balk at every—"

"Ah... I can see now why your company's so successful, Clare."

"Can you?" she said, having forgotten what she was going to say.

"I have no problem whatsoever imagining you as a strict headmistress."

He delivered it very tongue-in-cheek, his dark eyes full of an easy geniality. Clare couldn't blame him for teasing her, but she still flushed all over at his comment. She took a deep breath, hoping a fresh burst of oxygen would clear the miasma of longing that seemed to take over her brain and body.

A timely reminder to herself that Dev wasn't really the hero she was making him out to be in her head.

"I'm not going to apologize every time I have to advise you about your…sex life. In fact, to be on the safe side, I'd say, just don't have any. For a good, long while," she added feeling perversely petty.

Clare had never thought of herself as wicked, but the idea of policing Dev's sex life—because clearly the man was as distrustful of love as she was—filled her with delight. Whoever said there was a silver lining to every cloud was absolutely right.

CHAPTER FIVE

"EXCUSE ME? Did you actually order me to curtail my sex life?" Dev repeated her words, even though he'd heard her perfectly well. More importantly, he also agreed with her 100 percent.

The last thing he wanted or needed right now was to get embroiled with another woman.

He should have expected Sahara to show up after she'd told him she was in São Paulo. To network, she'd said, citing a renowned photographer that Dev was friends with. He had felt a little sorry for her when she'd lost her contract. But he couldn't help wondering if she'd felt anything for him at all. Or had he simply been a rich, powerful, good-looking walking, talking cardboard cutout of a man for her to drape herself over?

Can you blame her for that? a voice whispered inside his head. *When it's exactly what you want from your flings, when you pursue exactly the kind of woman who has no interest in you except your sexual prowess, your fame and your money?*

"Yes, I did," declared the woman in front of

him, dragging his attention away from the kind of thoughts he hated. Conscience-stirring thoughts that made a man weak and useless if he listened to them too much.

Clare continued. "As horrendously novel as this might seem to you, I'm the boss of you right now, Dev, until we fix this scandal and your image. Until we show the world that you're a wonderful, conscientious man who cares about women in the workplace, especially yours. I should decide who you see, who you talk to and who you kiss..." she declared, looking diminutive and delicate and decidedly ignoring the pink blush that crept up her neck.

Although there was nothing delicate about the steel in her words or the way she radiated a sort of resolute competence.

Even as she looked ridiculously cute in a makeshift dress styled from his shirt and belt. She was so much shorter than him that the hem of the shirt, thankfully, reached her knees.

Dev moved until he was standing at the foot of the few steps to the sunken seating area while she stood at the top. Her face still only came level with his, just. The wide-open collar of the shirt betrayed the rapidly fluttering pulse at the base of her neck. A prickle of awareness hummed to life under his skin. He studied the sharp curve of her jaw, the straightness of her nose and the blue shadows under her eyes that made them sparkle even more.

Her hair, cut precisely to enhance the line of her jaw, looked decidedly rumpled right now. His mouth twitched at the thought of the ever professional and polished Ms. Roberts sputtering away at the indignity of not being able to don the mask of ruthless efficiency she usually portrayed.

Once he'd had confirmation that there were some truly dangerous men chasing her—his head of security had even mentioned talk of a bounty on her head—he'd felt an immediate urgency to ensure for himself that Clare, with her larger than life smile and prickly demands, was kept safe from harm.

So instead of waiting any longer, he'd gone in search of her. And stared at her sleeping form for a full ten minutes like a horny teenager who was gazing at his first crush. She'd looked so fragile napping on the main deck, her mouth soft and lush in repose. Except Dev never normally felt the need to pursue women. Not since he'd shot up to his height of six-two at the age of sixteen. They'd done all the chasing.

And he wasn't going to begin now.

It was just that there was something deliciously delightful about riling up Clare Roberts for the simple fact that her blue eyes widened and her lovely little mouth gaped and a myriad of expressions crossed her equally beautiful face. All the while she processed her frantic thoughts and inevitably arrived at an affected indifference that even she herself didn't quite buy.

"So you're going to be like a twenty-first-century chastity belt," he added.

She scrunched her cute nose at the thought, reminding him of a proud, pretty little bird sticking its beak up into the air. But Dev didn't miss the quick sweep of her gaze over his lower abdominal region, as if wondering how such a contraption would work on him.

His nether regions, suitably impressed by her avid perusal, perked up with interest.

"Not quite, but if it helps you get the idea, I say run with the image."

Dev grinned. "I think you're taking your role in my life too far," he added, holding up his hand for her.

After a few seconds' hesitation, she took it. A jolt of sensation clamped him instantly, the memory of those delicate fingers tentatively exploring his body sneaking upon him suddenly. He let go of her hand as soon as her stiletto-clad feet hit the carpet.

"I'm absolutely not. Rich playboy billionaires are just as accountable to the verdict of the masses as we normal people are, thanks to the power of social media. Even a hint of one more scandal right now could be enough to start a domino effect. Believe me, Dev, if there's one thing I know, it's how to manage reputations."

"Fine, I'll try not to attract too many women. Especially if I have to disappoint them with a no access message to—" he moved his hand over his chest "—all this."

Just as he expected, her blue eyes widened and her lush mouth gasped with indignation.

"Shall we get back to the business at hand?" she asked pointedly, her chin lifting.

"Absolutely," Dev said, grinning.

Celibacy might not be such a hard concept with the enchanting Ms. Roberts to entertain him. Clare was so full of complexities that Dev couldn't help but be amused by her. As he settled down on the opposite side of the couch from her, he knew that she was precisely the right woman to fix both his personal image and that of his company.

To bring Athleta back onto the right path.

For all that he'd occasionally caught her gazing at him with a flash of desire, he believed that she would be all business. He could trust her. Dev had known that, even the first night he'd met her at the charity gala. Like all the big decisions he'd taken in life, he'd gone with his gut on that one.

It was why he'd broken his own rule and taken an unknown woman to his bed. Why he'd indulged himself so thoroughly when—despite all the spectacular stories the press wrote about his supposed indiscreet affairs with any woman he pleased—he never usually gave into his desires with such little forethought.

And while Clare fixed his image problem, he was determined to take a good hard look at the choices he'd been making for the last fifteen years.

That the man he'd trusted the most had been able to abuse not only Dev's trust but that of a woman in his employ was a direct consequence of the choices Dev had made years ago, while at military school.

Fueled by resentment and rejection, he'd set a goal for himself. And in the pursuit of that goal, he'd become bedfellows with a number of men whose principles he didn't always agree with.

Now he had achieved success and wealth beyond his wildest dreams. Maybe enough to even impress his arrogant father, with his ridiculously extravagant expectations for his children. As if they were all trophies and achievements to be polished and put on display instead of breathing, living people with flaws and dreams of their own.

And yet Dev had to admit to himself that somewhere along the path he'd chosen for himself, he'd lost his way.

He'd surrounded himself with people who courted success and wealth while trading in their principles. That had never been him—whether in his personal life or in business.

Which meant this was his chance to find the right path this time—he'd continue to build Athleta into the biggest and best sports brand in the world, but he wasn't going to do that at the cost of losing himself.

"What else is in your plan," he said, nodding at the glossy folder she held in her hands, "other than curtailing my…"

"…extracurricular activities?" Clare finished his sentence, picking up the thread of the conversation again. "Yes, of course."

She had no idea why she was this flustered. Dev wasn't even a difficult client. She'd had to put up with much worse, especially before The London Connection had yet to build the solid reputation it had now. And yet it was only Dev who again and again, tripped her circuits, for want of a better term.

Dev leaned back into the luxury leather seat, a devilish glint in his eyes.

"Right…" Clare opened her laptop and clicked onto the notes file she'd prepared earlier. "I'm just going to pull up this spreadsheet I created of the assets and liabilities we have to work with."

At that, he got up and took the seat next to her. The couch she was sitting on was large enough to provide ample space between them, and yet it felt as if the very air she was breathing was charged with the vitality of the man.

It took Clare a few seconds to focus on the list in front of her. She cleared her throat and then caught him trying to peek at her spreadsheet. "There aren't any secrets here, Dev."

"Oh, I know that. But it's interesting to see one's life so neatly reduced to two columns. I'm especially curious about the liabilities list."

Clare rolled her eyes. And thanked the universe for giving her the sense to remove that list from this sheet. "Don't worry. I'll handle your masculine sensibilities delicately. I know a thing or two about the male ego."

He laughed at that and the sound enveloped Clare. "Absolutely not, Ms. Roberts. Since you have curtailed any and all of my usual entertainments, this could be the only highlight of my week. Or even the month."

"What?"

"Getting dressed down by you for all my various sins."

Clare bared her teeth in a mockery of a smile. "No one was more disappointed than me at the blatant lack of those sins. I might have to write to the ruthless playboy billionaire club and have your title revoked. Instead of shadows of shady deals, all I could find was a veritable halo, which just needs a little polish." Clare didn't wait for him deny it. "We need to shine a light on the charity programs and drives that are sponsored by Athleta."

That mobile mouth narrowed into a straight line. "I don't give to various charities for publicity," he announced in an almost regal way. As if he expected it to be the beginning and end of the matter.

Clare frowned. Usually, with most of her clients—those with either old money or new—she had to work very hard to convince them that not every small bit of charity was something that could be used for PR. "Whether you give all these large amounts of money," she said, pointing a manicured nail at the figures, "for publicity or not doesn't matter anymore. The pertinent fact is that you do. *Give*, that is. Believe it or not, Dev, you're going to be one of my easiest clients."

With his arm snaked over the back of the couch, and his long legs stretched in front of him, she couldn't help thinking he reclined like a maharaja. The corners of his mouth twitched and that dimple—that damned dimple of his—winked at her again. "I do believe that that is the highest compliment you've ever paid me."

Clare snorted. "Don't go strutting around just yet. But, yes, it is. I don't have to manufacture reasons to show you in a good light. Or convince you that your charity work needs to be more than just a sop to your conscience. I've closely followed Athleta's charity work. It's why I wanted to work with you."

"You have made it more than clear that it's

only the job that's important to you, Clare. For the record, I'm no longer under any kind of misconception that you hid yourself on my yacht to seduce me."

Clare couldn't quite meet his gaze then. Knowing that he would see how horribly she was still attracted to him. Not that he probably didn't know.

Still there was a difference between him guessing and being given that information explicitly. "The world needs to know that Athleta is not rotten all the way through. That you, at the core of it, are still sound. That it was just one limb that was diseased and you quickly cut it off."

Any hint of humor disappeared from his face. "And I also severed everything that limb influenced," he retorted instantly. "Isn't that enough?"

Clare gentled her voice. Not just to appease the hint of bitterness she heard in his tone but because she understood where it was coming from. There was something very deep and complex going on with him, however much she wanted to continue believing that he was nothing but another shallow pool. "Would you give your trust back to someone once it was broken so easily?"

He looked away, his jaw tight. But as she'd known already, Dev was a man who faced the truth, always. Whether it painted him in a good light or not. Hand pushing roughly through his hair, he turned to face her, his dark brown gaze full of shadows that she couldn't see past. "No. I would never give my trust back once it was lost."

She'd meant to persuade him that it was going to take time and a little effort to convince the public, because he'd already, and had always done, the things that mattered most for a company's image anyway. But the vehemence with which he talked about his trust being broken... It found an answering echo within Clare.

"The various charities you give to—girls' education and empowerment through Asia, funding learning disabilities research in the US, youth scholarships for inner city kids... All these are things you and your company should be enormously proud of. It's not enough to do good, Dev. Especially now. It's also necessary to set an example. All the public normally sees is that you're basically living a life of extravagance and luxury and that you're this hot, athletic, aspirational figure that every average Joe wants to be and that every average Jane wants to be with."

Clare patiently waited for his laughter to subside. It wasn't a hardship because the man was insanely beautiful, and she was no better than the average Jane she'd just mentioned.

"You have such a way with words, Clare. You're very good for a man's ego."

Clare shook her head. "I'm not pandering to your ego at all. I'm trying to tell you that it's time to show people, especially your female employ-

ees, that you're more than some oversexed playboy billionaire."

He winced. "Oversexed playboy billionaire…
is that how you see me?"

Clare pursed her lips. Did the man intend to
jump on every little thing she said? "How I see
you doesn't matter at all. We're going to drip
feed as much information about Athleta's various charity activities as we can. Take this recent
visit to São Paulo, for example. What the world
thinks is you're here to party with some rowdy
friends of yours. And yet I know you came here
to work with a designer who uses recyclable materials for a new kind of sole for running shoes
and that you attended a conference that's address-
ing the preservation of the rain forest."

"You really have done your research," Dev replied, surprise in his tone.

Clare felt a pang of satisfaction. "I told you,
I'm very thorough when it comes to my job. The
next item on the agenda… We need to do an interview with Ms. Jones," she said, mentioning the
woman who'd exposed the harassment at Athleta
with enormous courage.

"That's out of the question." Dev looked as
if someone had punched him. "I'm not going to
hound the poor woman into giving a statement
just to make myself look better in front of the
world."

Clare leaned forward, determined to persuade him to see reason. "But what if she agrees? What if—"

"You've already contacted her, haven't you?"

Clare stilled at the outraged look in his eyes. "I'm not going to apologize for doing my job."

He sighed. "Fine. But I don't want Ms. Jones to be pressured in any way that she's not comfortable with. She's been through enough. Is that clear?"

"I understand."

"What do you suggest I do next?" he said, his brow still twisted into a scowl.

"We're going to do a couple of interviews on a sports channel and a major network channel with your sisters."

If she thought he'd been angry before, it was nothing to the fury that etched his face now. This emotion was not hot like before. This was icy cold, brittle, hard, turning his features from simply stunningly handsome to harsh and rugged.

With a curse, he pushed up onto his feet and moved away from the living area. She craned her neck up, her gaze hungrily trailing the economic efficiency with which he moved. The black trousers he wore clung to his powerful thighs, the white shirt highlighting his broad shoulders and lean waist.

She took the time to simply study him. He'd been blessed with inordinately good looks, and yet it was the energy with which he occupied a space that fascinated her.

It was several minutes before he turned back to face her, his temper firmly under control. "I was ready to agree to your suggestions because one of my employees wronged an innocent woman. But the responsibility for that lies with me, as CEO. There is no need to drag my family into this."

"But an illustrious family like yours can only be an advantage," Clare retorted, and then instantly wanted to pull her words back.

It seemed that her ill-thought words had only pierced anew whatever wound Dev was determined to ignore.

"Let's not get into the advantages and disadvantages my illustrious family has afforded me. It's above your paygrade."

The dismissal was clear and cold. She hadn't been lying when she'd told him that she'd handled a lot of difficult clients in her time. And yet Dev's dismissal stung her deeper than any other. It shouldn't have, considering their "business-only" relationship.

But she refused to let him railroad her, not in this. "I have no interest in digging into matters you deem forbidden, Mr. Kohli," she said haughtily. "But neither will I be told how to do my job. During my research, I discovered that your older sister is a world-renowned neurosurgeon and your younger sister is a state diplomat. We need to show the world that you're not intimidated by powerful women."

"Doesn't the list of women I've dated show that? I've dated several influential, wealthy women in their own right."

"No. That just shows that you're allergic to commitment and that you're pickier than a five-year-old when it comes to what he wants for dinner."

That shut him up promptly. Clare bit her lip to stop smiling. "At this point, it's not just that you and Athleta are being roasted everywhere. But have you wondered why your invitation to the Ethics and Equity in Sports panel has been canceled?"

"How the hell do you know that?" he said incredulously. "It's only just happened!"

Clare shrugged. "I have my sources."

"You don't have to remind me why I hired you," he said dryly.

"Then stop being so difficult, Dev. If you want to bring about change in your company, it has to start with you. No one said it was going to be easy."

"Are you charging me extra for the motivational speech?" he quipped. Humor was his default setting, Clare was beginning to see. But it didn't mean he wasn't hearing what she had to say.

"I'm just as excited as you are by the changes

you want to make. I've been out there, in the business world. The glass ceiling is very much alive and thriving, Dev. It's encouraging to see powerful men want to do their part in fostering an equitable environment for women."

"You're quite the force to be reckoned with, aren't you?"

"Why is there a question mark at the end of that?" Clare said, feeling as if the ground was being stolen from under her. It wasn't a bad sensation. Just a floaty one.

He frowned, his gaze sweeping over her features, as if he was searching for something. "Because there's one piece that doesn't really fit."

"What?"

"Why such a smart woman like you would make a deal with an unscrupulous Mafia boss. Even for much-needed capital. With your asset and liability columns and what little I know of you, I just don't see you taking a horrible risk like that."

Clare swallowed and gathered the papers she'd spread out on the coffee table in front of her. The unvarnished grain of the oak table felt like an anchor steadying her. She didn't know why she was hiding the truth from him.

Even Amy and Bea assumed she'd inherited the money after her dad had died, because the two things had happened so close together. She didn't know if it was her own fault for having foolishly trusted her father when he'd said he wanted to help her. She wasn't sure if it was shame or grief that sat like a boulder on her chest every time she thought of herself so full of hope and happiness when her dad had called her and she'd realized she'd be able to start her business.

She just couldn't.

"I told you. That was a naive decision I made." She switched off her laptop and picked it up. She was glad for the steadiness of her tone as she walked up the steps and faced him. "Both your sisters have already got back to me saying that they would be delighted to do it. I'll arrange for the interview through a virtual channel. I imagine that would considerably lessen the stress you're feeling at the prospect?"

He didn't quite give her the smile she wanted but that warmth flooded his eyes again. Clare felt as if she'd won the biggest lottery jackpot.

"Yes, thank you. Make sure any personal tidbits my sisters might mention are edited out. You're going to have a hell of a long conversation on your hands."

She nodded, intensely curious about his sisters, his family, everything about him. "And the contracts? Have they been looked over by your team of lawyers?"

An instant shutter fell over his expression. "Not yet. Don't worry, Clare. The contract is yours." He went on then, as if he wanted to fill the silence. "I'm having dinner in Rio de Janeiro to-morrow evening." His gaze did a quick survey of her, but didn't linger. "It might be a good idea for you to do some shopping in Rio when we arrive."

"Yes, please. Running away from a Mob boss and his thugs is the one disaster scenario I didn't pack for."

"Perfect. Then you can join us for dinner."

Clare's heart did a thump against her rib cage. "Join you? For dinner? You mean, as your part-ner for the evening?"

He shrugged. As if the matter didn't require further scrutiny. "I'm meeting an old friend and his wife, who's a notorious gossip. Showing up in front of her as my partner is like taking a front-page ad out that we're together."

"Together?" Clare asked, a totally unneces-sary, girlish flutter in her chest region. "Like a couple together? Or like a playboy and his PR guard dog together?"

Laughter lines crinkled out from the edges of his eyes as he threw his head back and roared. It was fast becoming one of her favorite sounds. "Your imagination needs to be put to better use than these scenarios you keep thinking up for us."

Clare straightened her shoulders. "If this friend's wife is such a gossip…"

"Then it's not a bad idea to fake it in front of her to help my reputation. A little smoke to start up a rumor that I'm falling head over heels with the mystery lady tucked away on my yacht…" He sighed when she didn't respond. "I thought being linked to me was what you wanted."

"For safety's sake, yes. But pretending in front of an old friend of yours is a completely different matter. Do you want me to flutter my eyelashes at you and simper?"

Dev grinned. "I'm sure you'll be found out in two seconds if you act all sweet and sugary toward me. Just be yourself—your starchy I'm-making-him-a-better-guy self who frequently likes to dress me down and keep my ego in check. Give your spiel about all the charity programs Athleta runs."

"To your friend?"

"I've been asking him to come on board with Athleta for a long time. This might be the push he needs since he's at a crossroads in his life too. I want to snatch him up before someone else does. He's a footballer and a world-class athlete."

Of course, business was at the center of everything for Dev Kohli. Still, Clare felt a flutter of interest at getting a bona fide glimpse into his personal life. "If he's a good friend, won't he know that we're just…faking it?"

"No, he won't. Especially once he meets you."

"And what does that mean, exactly? That I'm not up to the usual standard of your stunning girlfriends, so you must have lost your mind over me?"

Dev lifted his palms, a smile tugging at the

corners of his mouth. "Are you fishing for compliments, Clare?"

Her face heated, but she refused to leave it alone. "Of course not."

"Fine. You're just…different," he admitted.

"Different boring?" she pressed.

"Different…complex, okay?" His words had an edge to them now that Clare wanted to spend the rest of the evening teasing out. But that way lay nothing but trouble with a big *T*.

"Fine. I'll talk you up to him. It shouldn't be that hard. Although I don't see why you can't do it yourself."

"Is there anything worse than a man so pleased with himself that he won't stop boasting?"

Clare nodded, a shaft of pain hitting her in the chest. Her dad had been like that—he'd hardly ever called her, but on the few occasions he had, he'd never asked her about her own life. He'd always gone on and on about his next miraculous venture. Forever blowing his own, tarnished horn.

"I can have the chauffeur bring you back to the yacht after your shopping trip instead of joining us for dinner at the hotel, if you're afraid?" he taunted when she didn't respond.

"Of course I'm not afraid," Clare snapped, and the devilish man looked satisfied. He'd neatly cornered her into agreeing. "So are we going to stay overnight in Rio de Janeiro?"

"Yes. The next morning, we'll leave for St. Lucia."

"Okay. I'll meet you in the lounge for dinner."

"Can't wait to get away from me already?"

Clare sighed. "I'm not ungrateful. I just… I need to catch my breath. Can you understand that?"

"Yes."

"If one of your staff can get me a map of the city for tomorrow—"

He was shaking his head even before Clare finished her sentence. "That's not a good idea."

Something about his tone put her back up. "I've no idea when I'll get a chance to see Rio de Janeiro. I'm just going to play tourist. I won't be late and miss the dinner with your friend."

"I don't think you should venture out by yourself."

Fear gripped Clare. "Why? What have you heard?"

He shook his head again, but Clare had a feeling he wasn't telling her the complete truth. And that sent a spiral of fear and anger through her.

"I haven't yet figured out a way to solve your predicament," he said gravely. "Until I do, I'm… responsible for you, so I'll go with you."

She reached out to steady herself, her heart thumping dangerously loud in her chest. "I don't need anybody's protection. I certainly don't—"

"I can tell you're worried." His voice was curt,

commanding, and Clare held on to it. "You have dark shadows under your eyes. If you won't talk to me, talk to someone else. Family, or a friend… someone. Or you're just heading for a—"

"I don't have anyone to depend on, okay? I… don't want to worry my friends as they have enough on their plates right now keeping the business going without me. It's just me." Clare fought the sob building in her chest. She knew if she told her friends they'd leap to her defense and might get hurt themselves. They were better off out of it. But with his careful concern for her, Dev was determined to unravel her. "It's always been just me." Suddenly, she felt dizzy.

"Breathe, Clare." Dev's voice was hard in her ears, an anchoring point. "Focus on me, sweetheart."

Clare looked up. His brown gaze held hers— steady and reassuring. His hand reached out and took hers, enveloping her small one. The thump- thump of her heart felt a little slower now, as she focused on the line of heat his thumb traced on the back of her hand. The familiar scent of him wound around her, like a comforting blanket.

As panic misted away, Clare's first instinct was to snatch her hand away from his. The concern in his face, the gentleness of his touch…felt strange. Alien, almost. She wanted to shake it off and hide. To reject his simple kindness, which sent a lump swimming in her throat.

"Tell me what it is that you're hiding. And I can help you even more."

Her head jerked up. "Why?"

He looked adorably confused as he frowned. "What do you mean why?"

"Why do you want to help me? Other than the fact that I've thrust myself into your life as an unwanted stowaway on your yacht. The last thing I want is your pity. I need something real right now. Like I've never needed it before."

Clare didn't even realize she was speaking the words until she heard them. Until she felt him react by tightening his hand on hers. "God, I sound pathetic, don't I?"

"No," Dev replied. "You sound like someone who's struggling. Who's wary of leaning on anyone other than yourself. You sound…" He released her hand then. And Clare felt only desolation at the loss of his warmth. Long fingers squeezed her shoulders before he moved away from her. As if he needed to put physical distance between them before he did something he regretted.

"There's something in you that reminds me of…me," he said finally. "That's why I was drawn to you that night at the gala. It's why it felt like more than just another one-night stand. And why I had to walk away from you the next morning. Is that real enough for you?"

Clare stared at him, feeling a surge of something powerful in her chest. Her gaze traced the arrogant nose, the high cheekbones, the mouth that was always ready to laugh…his face was as familiar to her now as her own. She nodded automatically, hugging those unexpected words to herself. Still processing them… "I hope you're not pacifying me because you feel sorry for me."

He smiled and her world immediately felt centered again. "There's nothing about you that evokes pity in me, Clare. Exasperation, yes, but definitely not pity."

Clare laughed then, and if she'd had a better handle on herself, she'd have hugged him. Instead, she dipped her head, hoping to swallow the tears in her throat before they escaped. "Thank you. I've had a lot of distressing news of late and it…"

"Catches you out and brings you to your knees just when you thought you had a handle on it?"

"Something like that, yes," said Clare, stunned by his perception.

"Being strong doesn't mean you lean on no one, you know."

She scoffed. "This coming from a man who cuts himself off from the world on a gigantic boat?"

"Yacht," he corrected loudly, and then grinned. "It sounds like I've met my match in you," he said, regarding her with those brilliant brown eyes, as if he could easily see into her soul. One brow raised, and he muttered, "Come to me when you think you can, Clare, and tell me what fills your eyes with such grief. I swear it'll be our secret."

And then he bid her good-night. Leaving her alone in that warm, wonderful library of his. Giving her something that she hadn't even known she'd needed. The temporary respite from fear.

CHAPTER SIX

HOTEL FASANO—the latest playground of the uber-rich in Rio de Janeiro—kept its promise of the understated luxury and elegance that Clare had heard of and never thought of stepping foot in. The sparkling crystal blue of the ocean and the jutting peaks of the mountains calmed something inside her.

It was only when they'd alighted from the helicopter and Clare could breathe in the air that she'd realized how caged she'd been feeling. It wasn't Dev's fault or his yacht's. It was running from her own life that she detested.

If anything, Dev had only made her feel safer and more secure than she'd felt since she'd first seen the mobster's henchman dogging her steps in London. But the problem was, there were other things Clare felt compelled to run from. Dev, for instance.

Something about the concern and warmth in his gaze that felt far more dangerous to her well-being than any thug—her heart's naive longings that there could be more between them.

Clare flinched internally, aghast at her own thoughts and at the same time wishing she'd asked him to share more of his feelings about their night together. Wishing she'd delved deeper into the meaning of his words.

He was, she was coming to learn, quite a considerate man, for all that he tried to show the world only the shallow surface of himself. But just because he might be curious enough to know what secrets she was keeping didn't mean he had any special interest in solving her problems or healing the wounds inside her soul that never seemed to quite go away.

So she didn't like to give up control. Who did? Who was brave and foolish enough—in equal measures—to trust a stranger with their innermost fears? With their silly dreams that they should have long given up by the time they'd reached twenty-eight? Who poured out their inexplicable longings to a man who was stuck with her through no choice of his own?

Last night on the yacht, she'd snuggled into the sofa, not wanting to leave that library.

It was the one space on the entire yacht that had retained any of Dev's true personality. As if all the books remembered him. As if he'd left a warm imprint of himself behind after all the hours he'd spent in there. She hadn't wanted to be alone in her expansive cabin, adrift on the sea.

So, clutching a book to her chest, Clare had curled up and read and dozed. Noticed somewhere in that state between being awake and asleep that every book on the shelf also had an audiobook. Even some really old titles on subjects ranging from science and philosophy to Indian mythology.

On an impulse, she'd reached for a book on Hinduism and once again, there was its accompanying audiobook. Clare flipped through the book only to find that it was absolutely pristine. Each page still possessed an unmistakable crisp newness as if they hadn't ever been turned.

She'd examined older copies of some of the classics and it was the same. While the pages in those books were more yellowed, with the faint scent of aged paper emanating from them, it was apparent that they'd also hardly ever been thumbed through.

And yet, Clare sensed Dev's presence here— almost as if the books could tell her more about the man than he ever would.

Dev Kohli was anything but a one-dimensional playboy. At some point, Clare fell asleep, pondering the fact that it would be quite something to actually get to know him. Not that she could afford to.

She'd jolted awake to find herself cradled in

strong arms, the side of her chest crushed against a harder one. And the delicious scent of taut skin covering even tighter muscles invading her nostrils.

He smelled like Clare always imagined warmth and security to smell like.

Sleep heavy in her eyes, she'd looked up. Only to drown in that unfathomable gaze of his. Not even for a second had fear of a strange man holding her touched her. Even before her mind could completely grasp it, her body had recognized his. The strong line of his jaw, the wiry strength of his arms, the breadth of his shoulders…they had after all starred in her fantasy night.

And yet Clare knew it wasn't just her body that had recognized him, but her heart too.

She wondered if the thudding beat she heard was his heart or hers. Wondered how even in the slightly illuminated shadowy corridors through which he carried her, he could make her feel secure.

As she lay now, on a luxurious lounger next to the hotel's infinity pool on the eighth floor, looking out onto the beautiful Ipanema beach, supposedly glad to be escaping Dev's perceptive attentions, Clare was anything but escaping her own thoughts about the man.

Last night, as he'd carried her, she'd simply clasped her fingers tighter around his nape when it had felt like she was slipping out of his grasp.

"You have the habit of falling asleep in the most awkward places, Clare," he'd muttered, his voice husky and touched by sleep too.

A thick lock of hair had fallen forward onto his forehead. With no thought, Clare had pushed it back. Even after she'd done it, she'd felt no awkwardness. No regret or shame. Neither had his steps faltered even one bit. It had felt natural—her touching him so familiarly as if she had every right to do so.

Had he felt the same or had he simply not imposed that cold distance back between them because she was half muddled by sleep?

"I didn't want to be alone," she'd said, all her defenses down. He had seemed like a knight, come to take her away to a place of safety.

Clare cursed now, a flush claiming her skin. Where had her filter disappeared to?

"And the library is full of people?" he'd asked, a tiny line drawing his brows together. "Strange. I've always found it to be full of people's voices clamoring at me to hear them. So much to say, so much to teach…and always beyond my reach. It's like hearing the echo but never reaching the true source."

Clare frowned now, wondering at that cryptic statement he'd made.

"No, I don't think that, but it's not empty or soulless either," she'd said softly. "It's obviously the room you love most. Your presence lingers there."

His nostrils had flared, an enigmatic expression awakening in his eyes. "I don't know if I would quite call it love, Clare. I've always felt strongly about that room, yes. But it's not love," he'd said, a hitch of something—grief, pain—in his words.

Clare desperately wished she'd remembered more of the nuances now. She had this urgent feeling that he'd shared something extremely significant about himself. Something he wouldn't say in the daylight, in the absence of the intimacy and cover that the dark night and her sleepiness had provided.

She'd glanced up at him, his words puncturing a little more of her exhaustion. "Whatever it was, I didn't feel alone in there. Or afraid. I felt…safe."

His arms had tightened around her, more voluble than that gorgeous mouth of his. "I wouldn't think less of you if you'd simply admitted that in the first place, Clare." A soft smile crinkled the corners of his eyes. "In daylight, I mean."

She shrugged. "Care to show me how?" He was moving up steps now, and she was much more firmly held against his solid chest. If she hadn't been so intent on not disrupting the tidbits of himself he was tempting her with, she'd have nuzzled her nose into all that deliciously warm skin. "Because I learn best by example."

He'd thrown his head back and laughed then. And Clare had the weirdest wish that he would simply keep on walking forever and she'd continue to exist in that half-awake, half-aware state forever so that he would keep holding her and talking to her.

Which had prompted her to say, "Why did you come for me?" Hope and curiosity tied a knot in her belly. Hope that maybe he'd wanted her company too. That maybe he'd thought their night together had been remarkable.

"One of my staff heard you as they were coming to tidy up in there, and came to get me, rather than disturb you. You were having a bad dream. You kept saying, 'How could you?'"

And then he was walking into a bedroom and her heart fluttered like a bird caught in a cage.

"You're not alone, Clare," he had whispered then, gently placing her on the bed in a different cabin than she had been initially shown to. He had sat on the edge of the bed and held her hand—his large, calloused one enveloping hers like his body had done to hers once—and in that deep voice of his, commanded she go to sleep.

The traitor that her body was, it had immediately complied. She'd fallen asleep marveling at the novel quality of someone being there to comfort her, holding her hand to remind her that she was safe. Someone caring enough to say even those few words.

Mercifully, as far as she could remember, the night had ended there.

She'd woken up this morning in the vast bed, sunlight slanting onto her face. A quick look through the cabin had revealed the fact that she was now in a room that shared a door with the master cabin. Dev's cabin.

He'd taken her sleep-mumbled words seriously and kept her close by all night.

When she'd faced him this morning, Clare had refused to make eye contact. Embarrassment and something she couldn't define suffused her. That he had seen her like that…at her most vulnerable…it was a very uncomfortable feeling.

As if all that raw longing she sometimes felt inside was now on the outside for him to see. Her deepest, darkest dreams suddenly displayed in all their multicolored gaudiness.

But her fears that he might mock her or worse turned out to be unfounded. Because of course, Dev was the consummate gentleman.

He had perfectly followed her cue this morning, not even hinting at what had happened the previous night by raising his famously expressive brow. He'd simply asked her if she'd slept well. To which she'd focused somewhere over his shoulder and nodded.

So professional, the both of them.

When they'd arrived at the hotel, she'd gone straight to the boutique on the ground floor. Uncaring of the astronomical price tag for once, she'd bought a white two-piece bikini, as she'd forgotten to purchase one during her shopping trip beforehand. She'd desperately needed a little time to herself. Away from the shadow of the man who was beginning to pierce through her armor like a most determined arrow.

With her laptop in hand, she finished a number of administrative tasks and sent off a questionnaire to Athleta's newly revamped HR department. Looking through the interview questionnaire she'd prepared for Dev himself, she frowned.

He'd sent it back to her with a request to provide audio files of the questions. It wasn't that unusual a request, in the scheme of ridiculous requests that Clare had fulfilled for her clients.

But it made her think of the audiobooks she'd spied in his library aboard the yacht. How he'd said he couldn't immediately read and sign the business contract she'd put together for him based on the usual format she, Amy and Bea kept at the ready. How Clare had thought he was balking at the high price she'd quoted.

When she'd inquired if he was hesitating at how much her firm charged, he'd looked at her seriously. "Underestimating their own worth is often one of the biggest, most frequent mistakes women make in business."

Clare had nodded vehemently. "I learned that very early on in my career. And I never undercharge."

He'd just looked back at her steadily. "Good to know."

Clare had sighed and said, "That's not why you're not signing immediately then."

"No," he'd confirmed in a hard voice that didn't encourage further discussion. "But the contract is yours, Clare. Do you doubt my word?"

Clare had shaken her head. Knowing that to probe further was less than professional.

It had been a couple of hours before the straightforward contracts had been signed and returned to her. At the time, she'd thought he was just being very thorough with the vetting process.

Now, as she pulled out her phone and dictated the questions into it so she could email the audio file to him, Clare thought she was beginning to see the pieces of the man fall into place.

How and why he'd always played up the whole playboy role that the media had created for him. Why he'd trusted the man who'd betrayed him with so much power...

By the time late afternoon started edging into early evening and she needed to go get ready for dinner, Clare realized that however hard she'd tried to thwart her interest in Dev, it didn't make an iota of difference.

The more she learned about him, the more she wanted to know. The more she wanted to make this business partnership into something far more personal. But that way lay madness and hurt.

The sun was streaking the sky in shades of gold and orange, offering one of those unparalleled Rio sunsets that the city was so famous for.

The rooftop restaurant where she and Dev were going to entertain their guests, with its vintage retro lighting and buttery soft leather chairs and red brick facade, created an easy, intimate atmosphere. From the moment Dev had knocked on her door to escort her looking dapper in a casual jacket over tailored trousers, Clare knew she was going to enjoy the evening.

Neither had she missed the short but thorough appraisal Dev had given her sleeveless white sheath dress and suede pumps, and she'd had her hair styled at the hotel salon. Another expensive extravagance, but the warm admiration in his gaze was worth it.

"My friend has messaged to say they've been slightly delayed and we're to start without them."

After her hasty shopping trip when they'd arrived in Rio and the work she'd done poolside, Clare discovered she was ravenous once they'd been seated. She attacked the appetizer with a gusto she couldn't quite hide.

She looked up to find Dev's eyes on her. With his arm slung lazily over the back of her chair, he hadn't needed to bend too far to murmur, "I'm sorry if I embarrassed you, Clare. I was just…admiring your enjoyment of your food. You looked as if there was no pleasure greater."

The convivial atmosphere and the yummy food and that feeling of being free of thugs and fear—even for one evening—went straight to her head. And because some naughty imp was goading her, she murmured back, "There isn't. Except maybe the delicious weight of a man pressing down on…"

The sudden flare of heat in his eyes told her he knew what she'd been about to say. And yet Clare didn't feel any shame. Which was progress in her mind.

Dev was good in bed. He knew it. And more importantly, he knew that she knew it. It was high time she acted like an adult about it. Instead of looking like a blushing prude or imagining there was some sort of power play going on here.

Dev had never behaved as if this was a game to him. Even at his coldest. Which meant she needed to stop acting as if she was giving something away when she admitted how much that night had meant to her.

"Well, you know what I mean," she added in a breezy voice to cover up the sudden silence.

He didn't have to say anything as his phone pinged just then. "They're not coming."

"Oh…" Clare said, feeling a pang of disappointment. "Is everything okay?"

Dev shrugged. "Marriage problems I'd say. His wife can be a lot to handle sometimes."

Clare snorted. "Is that just conjecture? Or is there any truth to it?"

He sat back in his chair. Moonlight gilded the sharp planes of his features. "You doubt my word?" he said, mock affront lighting up his eyes.

"As a founding member of the playboy club, absolutely, yes. You might be the authority on everything else, but your commentary on marriage…sorry, but you're not likely to be an expert, are you?"

"I'll have you know I'm not against the institution of marriage, per se."

Hand on her chest, Clare pretended to gasp, "I don't believe it."

"I'm sure marriage is a healthy arrangement for people who want that kind of comfortable companionship and children. It's just not for…"

"Just not for you, of course," she said, rolling her eyes. "Why settle for one meal when you can have the whole buffet?"

He smiled, but when he spoke, there was something far from humorous in his eyes. "Those are your words, not mine. And please for all my sins, I'm not so bad as to declare there isn't a woman out there who's good enough for me."

"Then what is it?" Clare asked, unable to keep that question to herself. For too long she'd been wondering about him, and now, finally, here he was, the true Dev Kohli.

"Love requires something from me that I can't give. It's that simple."

Their gazes met and held, in a silent battle of wills. The breeze from the beach, the star-studded sky, with soft jazz playing in the background made for a beautiful night. But Clare knew it was this gorgeous man and the way he looked at her that made every cell in her body run wild. That, despite his professed inability to love, made him still so fascinating to her.

"Should we return to our rooms and finish some of the interviews maybe? If they're not coming, that is," she asked into the gathering silence. Just to bring herself back to earth. Just to cut through the warm cocoon of attraction wrapping around them. "There's still a lot to…"

"Or we could just enjoy the rest of the evening? You're a hard taskmaster, Clare." He raised a hand and their next course was discreetly placed in front of them.

Clare took a sip of her refilled glass of wine, to give her time to get control of her thoughts.

"Then you'll have to tell me a little about your swimming career."

"Don't you know enough about me yet?"

"Like I said, I'm building a profile of you for a few magazines. And I don't just want the stuff that everybody already knows. I want the real gold."

"And if there isn't any gold?" he asked curiously.

"Let me be the judge of that. Also, Dev?"

"Yes?"

"You have to trust me enough to know that I won't release anything you consider private information."

She saw him process that. Could imagine him loosening the boundary he held so rigidly around him. "What do you want to know?"

Clare leaned forward and smiled as she speared a baby carrot on her fork. "Tell me how you went from being a world-class swimmer to a billionaire CEO."

"That spans several very boring years."

"I've got time," she retorted.

He told her while they ate the rest of their meal. Peppering the details with funny anecdotes, self-deprecating humor, and more than a hint of anger and pain when he talked about the mentor in his company who had been the instigator of the sexual harassment.

"What about your father? I had a call from his

secretary about doing a joint profile on the two of you. As a head of the local chamber of the commerce, your father brings a lot—"

"Absolutely not," Dev said, immediately shutting her down.

"But he—"

"He never had a hand in making me, Clare. Except by forcing me to become a stranger to my own family. In making me doubt myself at every turn. He was instrumental in molding me into the cold, selfish man you have frequently called me. So, no, but I don't need his help in making me look good to the rest of the world, thank you very much."

The sudden silence in the wake of those impassioned words resonated in the air around them. Clare couldn't rush to fill it. Not when she recognized and understood the depth of anger and pain in them.

"I didn't mean to—"

"Don't apologize. That you eventually raised the subject of my father was inevitable. I should've just told you right at the start that he falls firmly into the category of forbidden topics of discussion."

"What will happen when you see him at Diya's wedding?"

"He'll finally see who I've become." The hardness receded from his gaze as he considered her sympathetic eyes. "And I have a plan to defuse any surplus interest in my family dynamics."

"Let me know how I can help," she offered automatically.

Clare saw a sudden flash of something move across his face. As if he was momentarily stunned at an insight he'd just had.

She had the most intense urge to ask him why he was staring at her like that.

She wanted to ask him about the audiobooks. She wanted to kiss him and ask him to kiss her again. She wanted to see those brown eyes turn infinitely darker as his passion was aroused.

She wanted to...

But she couldn't. He'd made it very clear that he didn't want the traditional dream of home and family that she still did. That he didn't believe in love or that he was even capable of it.

Clare shivered, even though the evening was far from chilly. In the next second, a jacket descended on her shoulders, smelling of his delicious warm male skin.

"Do you want to walk along the beach by the hotel?" Clare asked, turning toward him. "I recorded some questions for you about the press interviews," she added hurriedly. The coward that she was, she didn't want him to think she was asking just to prolong the evening with him. Even though she was.

If he thought she was acting strangely, he didn't

say so. "Of course," he said, his brown eyes twinkling. "Won't do for me to forget that you're only putting up with me for a paycheck."

Clare had no chance to answer as their lift door opened onto the expansive lobby of the Fasano where there was a tall, brown, insanely beautiful woman waiting in a peach-colored evening gown that clung to every curve.

"Dev? I thought that was you!" the woman exclaimed. "Oh, my God, I can't tell you how glad I am to have bumped into you…" She swanned across the marble floor toward them, the thigh-high slit in the gown showcasing toned legs that seemed to go on forever and ever.

Dev's mouth split into a stunningly warm smile. "Angelina…what are you doing here?"

He must have braced himself as she approached because he barely exhaled when she threw herself into his arms. Dev held her with what Clare could only call open affection. Angelina clasped his cheeks and kissed him, and Dev let her.

A strange buzzing filled Clare's ears. For which she was immensely thankful because it meant she couldn't hear the gushing words they said to each other.

She knew she should look away, or paste a polite, but inquiring smile on her face. Or just leave. But she did none of those. She simply stood there like some village bumpkin and stared at the bronze goddess, who must surely be a model, feeling as if someone had punched her in the middle.

Had she imagined a one-night stand, followed by an unwilling pity rescue from a nightmare situation, and one evening of pleasurable playacting at dinner equaled the beginning of something more meaningful?

Hadn't she learned her lesson yet about relationships and foolish dreams—the consequences of which she was still dealing with?

This was not her life, she reminded herself. This was a bubble she was living in until she figured out a way to escape the terrible fate that was threatening her.

Without a word, Clare turned away from them. If she could have sprinted to the lift as she was sure Angelina with her endless, graceful legs could have managed, she would have done so. Alas, she had to attempt to convey a dignified retreat on her wobbly, short legs.

"Clare, wait," Dev called behind her.

And since she couldn't just act like she was having a tantrum—even though she really wanted to—Clare turned around. A polite smile shimmered on her lips in its full fake glory.

His arm around the woman, he said, "I'd like you to join us for a coffee."

"Oh, must she, Dev?" The woman pouted, barely even glancing in Clare's direction. "It's not like you'll remember her name a week from now. I was hoping you and I could have a private chat."

"Clare's not one of my…" Dev suddenly stopped, staring at Clare, arrested. As if he couldn't find the words to describe their relationship. "She's…"

Their gazes held, an arc of electricity practically sizzling between them.

"She's what?" Angelina demanded, turning her curious gaze on Clare.

"What I am is very tired. I'm turning in for the night," Clare said, determined to remain polite in the face of the woman's horrible rudeness. After all, why should she be surprised? This was how Dev Kohli lived his life. "My body clock is still all upside down."

He nodded, and the suspicion that he'd only asked her to be nice was confirmed for her. Dammit, what the hell was wrong with her?

A thoughtful frown crossed his face as Clare met his gaze and then skittered away. "Okay. I'll see you tomorrow. We'll leave right after lunch."

Clare bade him a cool good-night.

And yet, as his broad shoulders disappeared into the lift with the woman still clinging to him, all she wanted was to go back and demand answers from him. Answers she had no right to. Because he wasn't hers.

Dev Kohli wasn't the kind of man who could belong to only one woman. Men like him and her father…they needed larger-than-life dreams, variety, constant thrills to challenge them. So maybe he wasn't the shallow, ruthless playboy that she'd initially thought him to be. But neither was he the kind of man who would settle for anything as pedestrian as marriage and children. And as much as she'd tried to bury all her dreams, somehow they always took root again in her heart—dreams of a man loving her forever, of building a family with him, of living the rest of her life surrounded by people she loved.

The thought of following the couple in the lift made Clare want to be sick. Instead, she squared her shoulders and stepped out into the night. At least a walk might clear her head of her heart's foolish notions.

Dev Kohli wasn't the man for her.

CHAPTER SEVEN

THE REPETITIVE BANG of a fist on the door to his suite brought Dev's head up. He put down the glass tumbler of whiskey he'd poured himself and opened the door.

Her face pale, trembling from head to toe, Clare stood at the entrance to his suite. She looked as if she'd been running for her life. "I'm sorry for interrupting your…date, but can I come in?"

"Yes, of course, you can, Clare," Dev said, pulling her inside. He slammed the door and leaned against it, his own pulse racing at the terror on her face. "What's wrong?"

"I… I went for a walk after you left with… her. Down to the beach. I wanted to clear my head… I…"

She swayed where she stood, and Dev reached for her. Clearly, she was in shock.

He slung his arm around her shoulders seconds before her knees gave way. That she didn't immediately protest made unease curdle in his stomach. He half carried her to the bar, hitching her against his side.

A burst of laughter from her mouth made him look at her, tucked neatly under his arm. There was a near delirious look in her eyes. "You should've been a football player. American football, I mean," she said.

Dev didn't know whether to smile or call for a doctor. "I considered that as a career for a while. I was told I was too small for it."

Another laugh. Less delirious but still with a slight hysterical edge to it. "You were too small? You…" Her gaze swept over his shoulders and his chest and trailed downward. And then back up again. She giggled, a sound that was very unlike the practical Clare he knew. "For what it's worth, in my opinion, you're very much not a small man."

Dev knew that fear had completely wiped away the cloak of control she usually deployed like some kind of invisible shield. Usually, he'd have preened at her admiring glance.

Picking up the drink he'd just poured himself, he held it to her mouth. She didn't quite sag against him, but he could feel involuntary shivers running up and down her spine. "Drink this," he said in a voice that didn't invite argument.

Scrunching that adorable, all too arrogant nose, she shook her head. "I hate whiskey."

"I don't care," he said, that tightness in his

chest releasing a little. The matter-of-fact way she'd spoken meant whatever had terrified her was slowly releasing its grip. "You've had a shock and you look…horrible." The pale cast to her skin, the whiteness around her mouth, it was as if all blood had fled from her face.

She grimaced. "Just what a girl likes to hear from the mouth of the man she's lusting over."

His gaze warmed with a heat that was never too far away when she was near. "I can see that shock is having other effects on you."

"I'm tired of acting as if I don't want you."

He laughed and pulled her closer. "Come on, Clare. For once, give in. The whiskey will warm you up, if nothing else."

She didn't argue further. Her fingers shook as she tried to take the tumbler from him. Dev didn't let go. He held the base of the tumbler as she tilted it up and took a couple of resolute sips.

She coughed almost delicately and gave the glass back. But he was glad to see some color climbing back into her face. His own pulse started slowing down from its former erratic pace.

"Now, tell me what happened."

Tears filled those blue eyes and spilled over as she raised them to his face. With a gasp of indignation, she wiped them off her cheeks. As if she found them beneath her dignity. "I think… No, I know I saw him on the beach, so I ran straight back to the lobby immediately and jumped in the lift."

"Who?"

"He got there just as the doors were closing." She closed her eyes, and sagged against the counter, as if her legs were giving out again. Dev tightened his hold on her. "That sweet smile of his… God, I'm going to see it till the day I die."

"Clare, who are you talking about?"

"Goon Number One, of course."

Dev didn't mean to laugh. Not when she looked like she'd shatter if he breathed too hard. But the way she'd said "Goon Number One," with distaste curling her lip, and her courage vying with her fear…he couldn't help it.

He was so surprised by the curse she spat out that it took a few seconds for him to react, and by then she'd slipped from his grasp.

Without having to turn all the way, he shot his arm out and pulled her back toward him. She landed against his chest, her forearms caught between them, blue eyes flashing daggers at him. "Let me go, Dev."

The fierce way she said his name made his pulse leap with excitement.

"Not so fast, darling," he said, adding an extra drawl to the endearment.

"I'm not going to stand here and let you make fun of me while I…" She shivered, as if on cue again. "I shouldn't have come to you at all."

Something about her reminded him of himself. She was clearly terrified and yet determined to hold her own. This woman was a fighter, just like him. No wonder she kept tripping him up.

Dev tightened his arms around her waist just as she fidgeted inside them. He pressed his mouth to her temple and she instantly stopped struggling. Her chest rose and fell, her breaths labored. He took his time, wanting to do this right. Knowing she needed exactly the right words from him just then.

Holding her like this, he could feel the strength of will it was taking her to prevent complete hysteria from settling in.

The scent of her skin—warmed by her signature lily-of-the-valley perfume—filled his lungs as he took a deep breath. "Take a moment, Clare. If you want me to let you go, I will. But right now, you need to be held. You need to know that you're safe. You need human contact—preferably male and large and able to provide at least an illusion of security. Ergo, someone like me."

Her laughing snort vibrated against his chest.

"I'll happily be the bad guy and hold you prisoner until you decide that it's okay to lean on me."

She whimpered then, and his muscles clenched as she pressed her open mouth to his biceps.

"For once, trust your instincts, Clare. Not your rational mind. You came to me because, despite the fact that you hate my guts sometimes, you knew you could trust me."

He knew firsthand how hard it was to be vulnerable in front of someone else. To let people see you in pain, lost, directionless. To hope that a kind word would be offered instead of humiliation or a tongue-lashing. And he fully understood her reluctance. From the very beginning, he had seen the similarities between them, the need to be strong in front of the world.

"I can't," she whispered, and the grief in her voice made him swallow.

"Of course you can." He pulled her in tighter and closer until her breasts were crushed against his chest, her legs tangled with his. Until he could rest his chin on top of her head and there was no gap between their bodies. "But until you can, let's just agree that I'm encouraging you to lean on me."

"Why are you being so nice to me?" she asked in a small voice that reminded Dev of himself on one of those bleak nights when he'd felt all alone in the world.

"Oh, didn't you guess already, sweetheart? I thought you had my number."

"I did," she whispered then, and he was glad to distract her. "But you keep shifting on me. I can't quite pin you down."

He smiled then, glad that she was too preoccupied to look into his eyes. He didn't like that she saw so much of him that he usually kept hidden from the world. From even his twin.

Slowly, ever so slowly that it felt like an eternity, the stiffness dissolved from her frame. Her breathing relaxed its harsh rhythm.

And then he heard the sniffle. The soft gasp that she swallowed away before he could fully hear it. He didn't let go. Only gave her enough room to adjust her head until her cheek settled against his chest and he could feel the dampness of her tears soaking through his shirt to his skin. For a man who'd always avoided emotional entanglements, he felt no urgency to restore the distance between them or to redraw their professional boundaries.

He had no idea how long he held her like that. He didn't care if an eternity passed. There was something about Clare Roberts that had appealed to him from the first moment he met her. And the more he got to know the different facets of her, the more he found her irresistible.

Eventually, the sniffles stopped and she let out a small sigh. But she made no move to tell him she wanted him to release her. So Dev didn't.

Slowly, seconds cycled to minutes and the air around them began to fill up with something else.

Dev became more and more aware of the soft press of her breasts against his chest. Of the heat radiating from the line of her spine as he rubbed his thumb up and down her back. The dip of her waist and the flare of her hips under his other palm. Of how small and dainty she was in his arms.

Sensation began to crawl back into his limbs and muscles, in the wake of that awareness. She shifted against him—rubbing her soft belly against his muscled one, and a dart of pleasure shot low into his abdomen.

"I wasn't laughing at you, you know," Dev explained, clearing his throat. Needing to puncture the building heat between them, he gently nudged her shoulders back until she wasn't touching him, so he could think straight again. "When you said Goon Number One, it felt like we were stuck in a…"

She didn't look up, but he felt her mouth open in a smile against his arm. The warmth of her breath felt like a brand on his skin through the thin material of his shirt. "In a nightmarish B-list horror movie? Believe me, I know exactly how that feels. Until I remember that man's smile and everything becomes all too real again."

"He's not going to get you, Clare. I'm not going to let him."

"I want to believe you. I do believe you. I just… How though? How long am I going to have to keep running? How am I going to—"

Dev tipped her chin up. After the tears, her eyes gleamed brightly. As if she'd come out on this side stronger and more determined. "You're sure it's him you saw tonight?"

"Absolutely. I'd give anything to be told that it wasn't."

Dev nodded. He had no reason to doubt her belief that the henchman had tailed her this far. Not when all his sources said the crime lord that Clare owed money to was a seriously dangerous man. Which meant it was time for action.

"You'll stay here tonight. In my suite. We can't take the risk of him nabbing you right out of the lift or even from your own suite."

She opened her mouth as if to argue and then closed it. With a resigned sigh, she nodded. Stepping back, she looked around his suite. Dev didn't miss the wariness that crawled back into her eyes. He knew she was looking for Angelina.

"I... I know that it's inconvenient for you to have me here tonight but I'll keep quiet as a mouse."

"I'm not sure if I can stay quiet however," some devil goaded him to say. "As you very well know, I'm quite voluble when it comes to..."

Her palm pressed against his mouth. "You're playing with me."

Dev tugged her wrist away. "Am I?"

"I jumped to conclusions, yes. The thing is I've never done this before."

"Done what?"

"Tell a man that I want to be the one he kisses.

Well, except for the last time. With you. Which was my first time."

He couldn't help but feel slightly shocked. She'd been so responsive he'd never guessed. "I know it's far too late for this, but I hope I...fulfilled at least part of your fantasy that night."

"You did," she said simply, and Dev knew she'd given him something precious and priceless. Something he wasn't sure he deserved.

It was just that every tentative smile and admiring glance that Clare threw his way had to be earned. It felt like he was constantly winning a prize—precious parts of her that she was reluctant to part with.

"Angelina is absolutely not my current squeeze, Clare. You ran away before I could clarify that. Plus, do you think I'd dare break the law laid down by you?"

"It's not funny," she said, coming closer.

His every muscle tightened with want as the scent of her reached him afresh. There was no hesitation or anger or reluctance in her gaze or in her steps just then. She looked as if she was determined to claim something for herself tonight. As if fear had washed away whatever kept her caged, instead of doing the opposite. She looked at him as if he was a prize. And yet he was nothing close to that.

"No, it's not. But you're determined to see me as some kind of rogue."

"You *are* a rogue. You're just not…" She looked away and back at him. There was a new light in her eyes, and Dev knew he should cut this conversation short right now. Knew that things were spiraling out of his control.

But damn it, the woman was irresistible. Even when she was busy thinking the worst of him— again.

"So she isn't your lover?"

"Nope."

Pink flushed her cheeks but she didn't shy from his gaze. His own humor came flooding back as he saw the inherent challenge in the lift of her stubborn chin. "It's just you did promise me that you wouldn't take any chances with your reputation right now."

Dev stared at how easily the damn woman shifted from terrified to assertive.

"So ask me," Dev said, lobbing the ball back at her. "You know you're dying out of curiosity. Ask me who she is, Clare."

If he thought she'd lift her nose into air and tighten that upper lip in fake haughtiness, he wasn't wrong. She did all those delicious things that made Dev like her so much. But she never ceased to surprise him.

Head held high, she demanded, "Who was that woman, Dev?" She looked like she meant to say more, but to his disappointment, she locked those words away.

She was standing so close now that he could see the pulse fluttering away at her neck. Could see the resolve glinting in her eyes.

"That was my best friend Derek Lansang's wife. The one that should have come to dinner with us. Not that I've ever gotten involved with a married woman, I hasten to add."

"She was very possessive of you."

Dev grinned, wondering if she knew how she sounded. "Angelina acts like that with every man she knows. It drives Derek crazy, but it's part of the woman he married. Despite their frequent spats, they do love each other. And I have some scruples, Clare. Just not as many as you."

Her shoulders ramrod straight, her gaze didn't budge from his even when she was in the wrong. Like Mama had done so many times. "I'm sorry. I shouldn't have jumped to that conclusion."

"No, you shouldn't have," Dev repeated, enjoying seeing her squirm.

Had she been jealous? Clingy, drama-creating women had never been his favorite kind, and yet there was something about being wanted by Clare that shredded his control.

"So that was Derek Lansang, the football player's wife," Clare mused. "I thought she looked familiar."

Dev nodded.

Blue eyes met his and held. "I was jealous,"

she said simply, and Dev wondered if he'd misheard her.

He had released his arms from around her, but her palms still clung to the material of his shirt.

"I… I had a lovely time at the dinner, playing your partner and I…got caught up in the fantasy of it. And when she appeared and you went off together like you were her knight in shining armor, I had this…most distasteful feeling in my belly. I know we laid down all these rules, and I have no right to feel jealous, but—"

Dev had never thought himself a man particularly prone to having an unruly heart. And yet something somersaulted inside his chest as he looked into her blue eyes. The lashes were still tinged with wetness and her straight nose was red; she should have looked ordinary. But the resolute strength of her character made her beautiful instead.

"But what, Clare?" he prompted, his voice hoarse.

"As I stood in that lift, I realized how sick I was of being afraid. How out of control my life has been ever since that man…started dogging my footsteps. How I've been just counting each day, longing for it to be over. How I've always tried to be the quiet, good girl who never demanded anything. Of herself or anyone else." And then she came closer and Dev could see the tremble in her lush pink lips. "I'm so angry. I'm furiu

about how much this bloody mobster is cheating me out of. I might escape him again tomorrow, but having this shadow always hovering over me, it's really not making much of a difference, is it? I could escape him every day for the rest of my life but still never be free."

"And that makes you mad?" Dev asked.

"That makes me…crazy," she said. And then her gaze focused on the now. On him. Dev felt his heart kicking like a mad thing against his rib cage again, and desire ran thick and heavy in his veins.

"So I've decided I'm not going to be scared anymore. I'm not going to simply lie down and give up. I'm not going to let every moment be consumed by fear. I'm going to seize the damned day."

"How?"

"For starters? I'm going to kiss you very thoroughly, as I've been wanting to ever since I woke up in your closet." Thick lashes flickered up and down his body before she met his gaze again. "If you're willing, that is."

Dev exhaled a long breath. Damn it, did the woman have any idea how arousing her artless honesty was? "Assuming I was—"

She cut his words off by trailing her fingers all over his chest. His heart pounded under her palm. The anticipation of a single kiss lit a fire in his blood like never before. But then some-

thing about Clare—that irresistible combination of honest, innocent passion, made his nerves sing.

"You are willing. That's all that matters to me. Yes, I already know your usual disclaimer. I don't care what this leads to or how long it lasts. I just want to feel this moment, live in it. Before all I remember about it is that I ran away from it. Before the only thing that will stay with me about this beautiful evening in this beautiful city is that… that bastard contaminated it for me."

She didn't leave it to chance. No, she hedged her bets to the highest, by tightening her fingers at the nape of his neck, going up on her toes until her breaths were crushed against his chest and she was burying her face in the hollow of his throat.

Dev's pulse pounded when she boldly touched her tongue there. Every muscle contracting on a wave of pleasure as she gently nipped the skin between her teeth. Every intention and rule he'd ever laid down for himself forgotten when she blew softly on the tiny mark she'd given him.

His hands on her hips tightened without conscious thought, and then he was pulling her even more tightly against him, until he knew she could feel his growing erection against her belly. She was gasping against his chin and then there it was…her luscious mouth against his—finally.

A stab of pure lust coursed through him as he dipped his head and pressed his lips to hers. Her moan fired up every nerve ending as he licked at the seam of those lips, suddenly voracious for more.

He reached for the round curve of her bottom with his fingers and hitched her higher against him. "Yes, please," she whispered against his mouth, and Dev lost the last bit of good sense he possessed.

As he delved deeper into the warm cavern of her mouth, as he tangled his tongue with hers, pressing her against the wall and drinking her in hungrily, the shape of the future—at least the immediate future—seemed to coalesce in his brain.

She needed his help. He couldn't turn away from the fact. So why not marry their problems and come up with the perfect solution?

He could show the world that he was settling down and changing his playboy image, and here was the perfect woman to do it with. If he felt a momentary doubt about whether he should be further involved with a woman who saw far too much of him all too clearly, it evaporated in the heat of their kiss. And anyway, not being tied down to any woman—even one as complex as she waswas his true nature. He'd be able to walk away afterward, just like he always did.

CHAPTER EIGHT

CLARE HAD LONG forgotten what it meant to feel vulnerable. If she'd ever known it as an adult, that was.

Once she'd been dropped off on her unwilling aunt's doorstep, she had, for the most part, learned to bury any emotional needs. She'd learned to keep her head down, work hard; in essence to be a quiet, good child with no demands. Either of her aunt or herself.

All the silly dreams she had kept building about her dad returning, though, she realized now were just those—something to sustain her through a barren childhood. As she had turned into an adult with little contact with him, she'd learned to foresee any need or want that might not be fulfilled and crushed it.

The need to be loved—unconditionally, of course—had to be the first one to die.

Vulnerability, she had realized long ago, was a costly thing for her. Her aunt had been the embodiment of the British stiff upper lip, and after a while, Clare had seen the value in it. But today, as she had walked away from Dev, while Angelina had wrapped herself like a vine around his broad shoulders, Clare had been drenched in a surfeit of emotions. As if everything she'd ever denied herself was determined to fill her up.

When Dev had opened the door to her, even through the spine-chilling fear, she'd felt the urgency to snatch what she could from life. To stop spending it burying herself in pros and cons. To put herself out there and live.

As Dev held her for his devastatingly hot kiss, fingers plunged into her hair, her body sang with spiraling pleasure. If only her every act of vulnerability could be rewarded in such a delicious way…

In the passionate depths of his kiss, she felt as if she was rediscovering the dizzying sense of being alive again. As if she was shedding layer after layer of all those sterile restrictions with which she'd caged herself. As if she was finally seeing the core of her own self on glorious display for the first time in years.

This had the potential to be as vivid and soul shaking as the fear had been. Except this was something she was choosing. This was something she wanted and needed and deserved.

This man and this moment and this…unparalleled, total joy in a kiss.

Pleasure suffused through her every nerve,

deepened by a giddy sense of power that he was just as mad for her taste as she was for his.

The shocking carnality of his kiss, because with Dev—a kiss was far more than just the slide of their mouths—it was a hungry, sensual exploration, a prediction of what their bodies could do for each other, and it rocked Clare to her soul. Every sweep of his tongue against hers, every nip of his teeth into the trembling flesh of her lower lip goaded her on. Every groan he let out filled the void she'd knowingly carved into her own life.

No more, she told herself. She was done hiding from life. Once she made up her mind, Clare had never been a passive participant.

The fabric of his shirt bunched satisfyingly within her grip. She snuck her fingers underneath, finding warm, delightfully taut skin. His powerful body shuddered when she raked her nails gently down his chest.

A fresh burst of desire bloomed low in her belly, urgent and grasping.

She set her fingers trailing up and down his chest and down to his abdomen. The clench of the hard muscle, the rough groan that fell from his mouth, the tightening of his fingers over her bottom…everywhere he touched, new pockets of sensation opened up.

There was already a familiarity to how they touched each other. A languid understanding of what the other craved, a rhythm to the give and take they engaged in. Clare delighted in this knowledge. And she used it ruthlessly, no longer bound by her own confining rules.

That first night they had spent together a few weeks ago, she'd let him take the active role. That was nowhere near enough for her anymore. She loved the light dusting of hair on his chest. She wanted to lick the hard slab of his abdominal muscles.

Why had she denied herself the life-affirming sight of that happy trail?

She wasn't going to let the mobster win. She wasn't going to let her father's cruel neglect of her or her aunt's cutting indifference define how she lived the rest of her life. "I've wanted to do this again," she said against his mouth, "ever since I woke up next to you that morning. And now I can't think of one good reason why I denied myself. I wrapped myself up in so many layers of protection that I lost myself. No more."

His hands moved up from her hips to her shoulders with a possessive thoroughness that pinged every cell in her body. Slowly, with a long, rough exhale, Dev pulled back from the kiss. "No," he agreed, his thumbs tracing over her cheeks in an almost tender gesture. "Nothing has ever tasted as sweet as you, Clare. Or been as full of surprising depths."

"Are you complaining?" Clare said, burying her face in his throat again. She loved the rough, bristly texture of his skin there, the taste of him, the scent of him. It was beginning to feel like her safe space. But of course, he wouldn't appreciate it if she said that.

He wouldn't like it if she took this interlude as anything more than what it was—a fragment of time where he was letting her set the pace and tone of this.

One kiss. Not that she'd had any doubts about his desire for her.

His fingers edged into her hair at the nape of her neck, his thumbs rubbing in mindless circles. "Not at all," he said. "Nothing but admiration here."

"Lower please," she said, in defiant demand.

His laughter vibrated through his body, transferring to hers. "Yes, my lady." He obediently moved those clever fingers down her neck and onto her shoulders.

Clare groaned when he pressed them into the tight knots he found there.

He was unraveling her, she knew. On more than one level. But she had no energy to resist. No wish to erect her silly defenses.

"Why?" she asked, wanting to know everything he thought of her.

Now his fingers were gently kneading her arms and her back muscles and reducing her to a blob of good feeling and nothing else. "Why what?"

"Why admiration? Because I kissed you better than I did last time?"

Again, that laughter. It was low and warm, and it made her chest feel full of a comforting quality. Clare wanted to roll around in that sound forever and ever.

"Why not? You took sheer terror for your life and transformed it into passion and determination. You didn't let it diminish you. You used it to find a new you…that, lovely Clare, is cause for admiration and celebration."

Clare clung to him, no inhibitions or reserve left in her. She'd worked hard all her life with no boyfriends or thought to the future except establishing her own business. The money her father had "given" her before he died—at such cost— had finally allowed her to do that. But the driving force had been her determination to build something for herself.

"You know something about dwelling in fear and forging something out of it, don't you?" she said then, knowing that she was crossing that invisible boundary she'd always sensed around him. Knowing that he might put those walls back up again in the beat of a breath and shut this interlude down.

But she was tired of being circumspect. Of settling for less than what she wanted.

She was also aware that patterns built over a lifetime of abandonment couldn't be broken overnight. Sooner or later, she was going to revert to her old habits. To being circumspect with her emotions. To becoming one of life's spectators once again.

But in the meantime, she was simply going to look at this as a forced, but much-needed vacation. And the main feature of her vacation would be doing deliciously wicked things with Dev Kohli.

Pupils darkened, mouth swollen, hair in disarray, the man looked scrumptious. There was none of that suave, unruffled playboy right now. This was a man in the throes of hard lust. She liked seeing him like this—all gorgeously rumpled, thanks to her hungry kisses.

If she could throw off her shackles for anyone, it had to be this man. Who, she was beginning to suspect, was quite the package—inside and out.

There was a sudden pause, but he didn't push her away and tell her that asking such a question was above her paygrade. Or that their devastatingly sweet kiss didn't give her a right to delve and probe.

Instead, he drew in a long breath and Clare felt the echo of it in the rise and fall of his chest. "Yes, I do know what it feels like when no one hears you. Or sees you. I know what it feels like when the only definition you have of yourself is set by others."

Clare gave up all pretense then. She threw her

arms around his waist and held on tight. His large hands moved over her back—in an act of appeasement or need, she had no idea—and then he pulled her close.

"You're a witch," he said gruffly, but his fingers were gentle as they clasped her cheek, and then he was kissing her again.

This kiss was not gentle or sweet or exploratory. It was a fierce taking. It was a toll he demanded for giving a piece of himself. His fingers clasped her bottom, holding her firmly against his hard body, his erection a brand against her belly. Clare felt the most overpowering need to touch herself between her thighs, or beg him to. The ache that built there was so insistent.

"I want more," she said brazenly, determined to ride this high for as long as she could. She could feel a flush climbing her neck at her pouty request, but she didn't care. "I want a repeat of that night."

His sudden curse ripped through the air.

Hands on her shoulders, he gently put her back from him. "Let's think this through for a moment, Ms. Roberts. For one thing, you're in shock. For another…" His brown gaze zeroed in on her lips, and he seemed as though he'd forgotten what he was saying.

Clare licked them, wanting to feel the swollen sensitivity everywhere else too. "Lost your train of thought there, Mr. Kohli?"

"I think first we both need a cold drink and then… I suggest we wait." Another sweep of his eyes over her body, and it was almost like those big hands had stroked her all over again.

Her gaze dropped down. The outline of his erection was clearly visible. An incredible rush of female empowerment hit Clare in her belly. She flicked her gaze up to meet his eyes. Saw desire etched onto his sharp features. "Why wait? I told you, Dev, you don't have to worry that I'll ask for more."

A flush streaked the sharp blades of his cheekbones. "It's not that. We need to discuss something important first. I think I've come up with a way to get you out of this."

"Out of sleeping together?"

A smile split his mouth. "No." He rubbed a hand over his face. "I think I've already made my peace with the fact that you and I'll end up in bed again soon enough."

"That confident of your studly prowess, huh?" Clare interjected, wanting to be miffed but not really succeeding. She couldn't pretend anymore that he was simply a man who looked at women as conquests or mindless entertainment. Neither was she going to turn him into perfect relationship material with her overactive imagination.

The present was all she had, and she was going to revel in it each day she could.

He shrugged. "Not my studly prowess so much

as chemistry like ours. It doesn't happen all the time, and this is the strongest I've ever felt. Does that answer satisfy you?"

His tone glinted with humor and challenge, and Clare nodded regally. The answering warmth in his eyes made her heart feel too big for her chest.

"Do you get the sense that our roles are being reversed?" she said then, pulling away from him.

But he didn't let her hand go. Clare's heart jumped at the small gesture that had nothing to do with desire or lust and everything to do with something else. Something she didn't want to define. If she gave it a name, there wouldn't be the chance of an escape. "What do you mean?" he asked curiously.

"Like I'm becoming this devil-may-care woman and you're—" she smiled, loving how he tilted his head and stared at her hungrily "—turning into some kind of honorable man trying to keep me out of trouble."

Dev laughed. "Am I? Don't worry, Clare. This whole honor thing will wear out soon enough. Just listen to me, first."

Clare nodded, a trickle of apprehension diluting the heady sense of excitement that had filled her. She didn't want to face reality just yet. She didn't want to turn into boring old Clare again.

She liked this new, fun, to-hell-with-everything Clare she got to be with Dev. There was something about him that had made her want to push herself, from the first moment she'd laid eyes on him.

A smile creased his cheeks and that damned dimple flashed at her. "Don't look so worried. This should get you out of the Mafia thug's hands permanently."

Her pulse zigzagged through her body. "How?" she demanded.

"We'll simply get married."

Simply get married...

It had sounded simple in his head but as he watched how his suggestion landed on Clare, Dev wondered if he'd made a big mistake. Not about wanting to protect her. One way or another, he was going to get her out of this predicament.

He'd always had an affinity for the underdog. Seeing that he'd been one himself. Or at least he had before his transformation into an...*an oversexed playboy billionaire*, as she'd called him.

His mouth curved at the title.

While he still didn't understand how a smart woman like Clare could have made such a bad error in judgment by borrowing money from a known mobster, he couldn't hold it against her. His company wouldn't have been in this giant mess if he hadn't made a ghastly one himself.

But...given the way all humor fled her face at his words, and the way she stared back at him, he wondered if he'd just made another error.

By assuming that she'd take his idea in her stride. That she'd see it only as a solution to her problem and not something else. Something more.

When several minutes passed and she still didn't say anything, Dev felt more than a hint of irritation. "Do you have a boyfriend tucked away in London who might object to this idea?"

He knew it was the most ridiculous question the moment he heard it. She'd never hinted at any prior relationship, and he'd gotten the sense that Clare kept her relationships carefully vacant of too much attachment. But...the words had stemmed out of jealousy. From a place he didn't even know existed.

Which was ridiculous. Because it wasn't as if he was asking for anything from her, during their proposed arrangement. Nothing that wasn't inevitable anyway.

The very inelegant snort she let out told him the same. "Of course I don't." Then she straightened and he could see anger building in her face. "Do you think I'd be...cavorting around with you if I had someone I loved back home?"

"Cavorting?" he said, raising a brow, hoping to deflect her attention away from his stupid question.

"Don't think you can distract me, Dev," she said, putting paid to that tactic.

"Then what's the problem?"

She took in a deep breath. "The problem is

that marriage is a big step. I…it means a lot of big things like trust and fidelity and…"

Dev reached out and rubbed a finger over her cheek. "I do trust you, Clare. Which is why I'm not hyperventilating."

She looked him up and down. "Are you the type to hyperventilate?"

"If the topic of conversation is marriage, yes. Does that make me less manly?"

"Nothing makes you less manly, Dev," she snapped, with more than a bite to her tone.

"Ah…so the hyperventilation would be a symptom of the underlying condition of not wanting to commit, is it? I forgot that you're the founding member of the bachelor playboy club, allergic to all things long term."

He scrunched his nose in distaste. "You make me sound like I have a disease. But no, a traditional marriage isn't in the cards for me." He pushed a hand through his hair, annoyed that she kept making him ponder things he'd never… well, pondered before. Like marriage. And fidelity. And long-term relationships. And how it would feel to have someone permanent in your life who knew you inside out. Who would make you laugh and want and push you to be a better version of yourself.

Who would also have complete control of your emotional health? Who could destroy your self-

worth with one well-targeted barb? the sanest part of his brain pointed out.

No woman was worth opening himself up to that kind of risk again. Yes, that meant sometimes his life was lonely. But it wasn't exactly a choice he'd made so much as a defense mechanism. A way he could survive intact. The only way.

"And while, yes, this is bigger than anything we've both done, it is to our mutual benefit."

"How?"

"Firstly, it should stop this mobster from just… taking you. As my wife, you'll be so much more high-profile, and there will be permanent security in place around you. He's unlikely to just kidnap you, which gives us time to negotiate and see if paying off his loan is going to satisfy his desire for vengeance. As for me, it provides me with instant respectability. A distraction for the media to focus on while I sort out Athleta. It's getting tiring hearing my competitors using this scandal to try and get ahead of me. My twin called and told me both my sisters have had paparazzi chasing them. Diya's also had to put up with my dad's lecture about how I'm casting a shadow over Bhai's shining reputation."

"Bhai?"

"My older brother," he explained. It had been only a matter of time before Dev heard his father's opinion on this matter. It didn't mean he'd ever been prepared for it.

"I told you those interviews with your family were important," Clare said, mercifully interrupting the spiral of anger and frustration he got pulled into whenever he thought of his father. "People need to see your face alongside theirs. They need to see different sides of you."

"I agree. And this way, they will see not only a loyal brother, but a happily married man—head over heels in love with his wife. Two birds with one stone... It seems to me like it's the best stopgap measure."

She laughed and Dev sensed the ache she couldn't hide in her words. "I never imagined I'd hear the words 'stopgap measure' in a proposal."

"Does that mean you've imagined getting a proposal?"

He thought she'd shrug and laugh it off. He needed her to. He didn't want to discover at this stage that Clare was the romantic type.

"In a faraway future kind of way, yes. I'm a businesswoman through and through. But it doesn't mean I didn't harbor the hope of a husband and a family someday. I want to be a wife. And a mum." She swallowed and looked away. When she turned and look back at him, her blue eyes glittered in a way he'd never seen before. "I want to belong. To someone. To something. I've always wanted more than just a career."

If she'd kicked him in the chest, Dev would have been less surprised. He didn't know why.

He'd heard her talking about her best friends. He'd seen the hurt on her face the morning after their incredible night together when he'd told her they were done.

But somehow he'd thought she'd be more like him. More disinclined to take the traditional path in life. The idea of Clare marrying some stranger and having his children did strange things to his insides. Things he didn't want to dwell on.

He had to make one thing clear. "You're only in your twenties. All those things are still possible for you, Clare. This marriage is only a temporary solution to both our problems, and it doesn't mean you'll have to give up any of your long-term dreams."

"Making sure I know the score?" she said, the earlier ache in her voice gone. "Making sure you're in the clear? Don't worry, I understand."

He should have been glad that she could so easily shelve her hopes for the future. That she could keep that part of herself mostly hidden. Instead, Dev only tasted a perverse bitterness that she'd so clearly decided that he wasn't going to be included in that particular dream.

Even though, that was exactly what he'd already warned her.

He shrugged. "Earlier, on our way to the foyer after dinner, I spotted a photographer from a popular lifestyle magazine watching from behind one of those giant trees in the courtyard when I was giving you my jacket. I have a feeling the shot he took was quite an intimate one."

She gasped. "Why didn't you stop him?"

"It was too late," Dev said with a shrug. "I'm sure that photo of us has already hit the internet. There'll shortly be rabid speculation that I have a new woman. In a day, they'll know it's you. This way, we're staying ahead of the curve and dictating the news. We could get married at my villa in the Caribbean, and by the time we've sailed back to California for Diya's wedding, the news of our own private, top-secret wedding will be all over the news. As I've already said, hopefully, it will at least make your mobster think twice about snatching you openly. Between us all, my family has a lot of clout."

"He's not my mobster."

"You know what I mean."

"And it will only be an arrangement of convenience?" she said cautiously.

Dev nodded. "It can be whatever you want it to be, Clare." He pinned her with his gaze. "Do you trust me?"

"I do." Her instant answer calmed the furor in his head. Dev kept seeing the damned image she'd created in his mind—Clare marrying some staid accountant type. Clare running behind two children. Clare in bed with this boring old accountant who was nevertheless extremely good in bed.

Or was that himself he was imagining in her bed now?

Dev cursed.

Her gaze held his, a question in it.

Dev shook his head.

"I have a few conditions," she said after what felt like a weighty silence.

"Whatever makes you more comfortable," he said.

"I would like for us to have a prenup."

Stunned, Dev stared at her. It was something he'd fully intended to work into the conversation. With wealth like his, they were as common as summer homes in warm places. But it had felt somehow wrong discussing one with Clare. As if he was questioning her character.

"I'm glad I can still shock you," she said with a small smile.

Dev said nothing.

"I…when this is all over—however long it takes—I'd like to part as friends, Dev. I… I don't have a lot of those but the ones I have, I like to keep them. A prenup guarantees that our divorce will be straightforward, and we'll be more likely to keep in contact, right?"

"If I'd thought otherwise, even for a moment, I wouldn't have suggested this."

She nodded. "I'm realizing that."

"Is that all?" he said, uncomfortable with the look she sent him. It wasn't exactly gratitude.

It was the same thing he'd seen in her eyes that morning. And the night when he'd carried her from the library on the yacht.

It was an emotion that Dev didn't know how to accept. Or even how to feel it himself, much less return it.

"Will you have loads and loads of marital sex written into the prenup?"

Dev didn't laugh. Because as sure as he was that she was serious, he was also beginning to understand that this was no small matter. He held out his hand to her.

She looked at it without taking it.

"Come, Clare. Let's get you to bed. You're in shock and I shouldn't have sprung this on you."

She shook her head stubbornly.

"You're angry with me, I get it. We can talk this over after you've had a good night's sleep."

"I'm not angry with you at all. You're going above and beyond for me. It's just... I have a hard time being dependent on anyone. I don't want to be beholden to you, Dev. At the same time, I don't think I can quite act per some guidelines written down on paper. It would be too much of a farce. It would make it as much of a cage as that mobster was wanting to thrust me into."

Dev held her loosely, her fierce need to be in control of her own destiny striking an echo in him. "What can I do to make this better for you, sweetheart?" he said, pressing his mouth to her temple. "What can I do to make this less a punishment and more of your choice? Other than the lots and lots of sex that we're going to get to have during this marriage, that is."

She laughed then, and he felt as if he'd won a gold medal again.

As if for the first time in his life, there was perfect alignment, perfect harmony between him and another soul.

It was also the first time in his life he'd laid himself open and offered to give someone else everything he could. Emotionally, that was.

CHAPTER NINE

DEV KEPT SURPRISING HER. In a good way. In a fantastic, knee-buckling way. In a come-trust-me-with-your-heart kind of way.

Clare was so tired of freeze-locking her heart. Of pretending it didn't want more. That it hadn't already started thawing in this man's presence a while ago.

She was so tired of pretending that she wanted more out of life.

She looked into Dev's eyes, something solid and immovable lodging in her throat. She kept expecting so little, and he bowled her over every single time. A strange swooping sensation began in her belly, as if she was perpetually in flight. She drew a deep breath. "I need this to be more than just a…sterile agreement on paper."

He curled his upper lip in a deliberately lecherous way. "You mean all the sex won't unsterilize it? Because if I remember rightly, it was explosive."

Clare laughed and tucked away a lock of hair

that fell onto his forehead. There it was again—
that floaty feeling. It felt like the most natural
thing in the world to laugh with him like this.
To touch him like this. "Like you said, we'd have
done that eventually whether we got hitched or
not."

"True," he said with a nod. He sat down on the
sofa and pulled her onto his lap with an effort-
less poise, as if he couldn't go too long without
touching her. "Let's see then." His palm was big
and broad against her back, and Clare wanted to
melt into it. "I prefer to sleep in the center of the
bed. And I hog all the sheets."

Clare slipped her arm around his neck and settled in. "I would have found that out anyway."

He grinned. And tangled his fingers with hers
in her lap. "So this is like a toll I have to pay
then?" His thumb rubbed at her pulse on her
wrist. "For you to marry me?"

They were both smiling and he was touching
her so casually, and yet Clare could sense that
invisible boundary tightening around him as he
spoke. But she wasn't going to give in and let him
keep his distance from her.

It had nothing to do with their getting married
either. It had everything to do with the fact that
she wanted to know more about him. That she
wanted him to share in her own life too. That for
the first time, she wanted more from life itself.

The strength of that urge sent a shiver of fear

through her. An almost familiar echo from when she'd so patiently waited for her dad to show up, although he never did. But Clare pushed it away.

"How about I share something first?" she prompted, not for a game of give and take but because she wanted him to know. Because he'd earned her trust. By giving his own to her.

He looked at her and knew. Just like that. He knew from her face that it wasn't a small or silly thing. "Clare, it doesn't—"

She pressed her finger against his lips. "I want to tell you this." She swallowed the ache in her throat. "I haven't told a soul since I found out. But I want to tell you, Dev."

His fingers tightened over hers. "I'm not going anywhere, sweetheart."

"I didn't borrow the money from that crime lord. In fact, the first I heard of him owning me—" she shuddered, and Dev's arms came around her like a cocoon "—was when that goon of his accosted me in London. I didn't take the money, Dev. I didn't even know who he was."

His finger under chin, Dev tilted her face up to his. "Then why does he think he owns you?"

Shame filled her chest but Clare pushed on. "My father passed away a few years ago now. We…we were not a normal family."

"Is anyone's family normal, Clare?" he said, and Clare heard the answering ache in his words. It made it so much easier to go on.

"I have no memories of my mother. When I was five, my father dropped me off at my aunt's. With loads of promises of coming back. Of traveling around the world, making his fortune and treating me like a princess."

Dev nodded, encouraging her to go on.

Clare laughed, feeling that hope and disappointment in her chest like it was yesterday. "My aunt was not happy, to say the least. But she gave me shelter and food and for the most part, she was indifferent to my existence. But I hung on to my father's promises. I believed that one day he'd come back for me. It sustained me...that hope."

"But—"

"If you say it was foolish, I'll never forgive you. So please don't."

"I won't," he said with emphasis. "I won't say anything you've done is foolish, Clare. Or wrong. You're a survivor. That's all that matters."

Clare thought she might have fallen a little in love with him then. "I studied hard, got a scholarship to go to an excellent private school. That's where I met Amy and Bea. I found a job I liked, but I always wanted to be my own boss. So one day, Dad contacted me to tell me that he'd discovered he was dying, but that his hard work had finally paid off. That he was sending me a sum of money that I would have inherited after he passed away anyway. He said it was his gift to me—reparation for all the birthdays and holidays he'd missed. I was overjoyed to hear from him after so many years, and devastated he didn't have long left to live. I was foolish enough to think my faith in him had been validated. It was a lot of money, and I used it to set up The London Connection."

Dev's brows pulled together into a ferocious scowl. The tension in him was immediate. "Wait, so he sent you that capital? He took the money from the mobster and gave it to you?"

Her eyes prickling with heat, Clare nodded. "I wondered how that even works, in this day and age. Yes. And of course he died without paying it back. So the mobster eventually discovered what happened to him, and turned his attention to me. How could a man use his own daughter as collateral? Did he think a major crime lord would never find me?"

"I'm so sorry, Clare." His hand around her arm, his mouth pressed to her temple, Dev held her tight. As if he was determined to stop her from falling apart.

"I keep thinking with each day that passes, it'll hurt less. That I'll understand why he did this. That something will make me see the whole thing in a new light. But the cold, hard reality doesn't change. When all his other schemes failed, he took the easy way out. He only sent me that money before he died to salve his own conscience for neglecting me my whole life, and he even managed to mess that up in the worst possible way."

I took money from a man I shouldn't have trusted.

Her words came back to Dev. She'd meant her father, not the mobster. How could anyone hold that against her?

Dev fisted his hands by his side, fury filling him slowly. What the hell kind of a man jeopardized his daughter's life like that? He banked the fury knowing that it had taken Clare everything to tell him that much. Knowing that she needed comfort just then and nothing more.

She didn't want a champion; that much had been clear from the start.

But this... Dev now understood the fear, the need to be in control, the strength of will it had taken her to not only manage her emotions but to use the opportunity to pitch her firm to him.

Having always lived in the world of over-achievers, Dev was full of admiration for this woman who'd withstood so much and still remained strong and fierce. All the while retaining a sense of joy in life.

"It's not your shame. Or even your burden, Clare. It's his. It doesn't matter that he repeatedly broke your faith in him. That he betrayed you in the worst way possible. None of it is your fault. You know that, right?"

"I do know that. But I've moved on from anger and hurt. I have to."

Dev frowned. This woman was forever going to surprise him. "What do you mean?"

Clare shifted her head and met his gaze. "If I let it, what he did will become a poison inside of me. It will corrupt my business, my life, my heart. And that isn't something I can afford to allow to happen. I have to choose to forgive him. Or it will become the thing that will consume and corrupt me." She took a deep breath. "So I'm going to try to let it go. I'm going to focus on getting out of this mess. On moving forward with my life. And that means I'll marry you and help polish your tarnished halo—" she scrunched her fingers through his hair, and his scalp prickled with sensation "—playing the part of your adoring wife for a while...and then go back to making The London Connection even better than it already is. There, now I feel mostly in control of this situation."

Pleasure and pride wound through Dev like a rope that couldn't be untangled. At the same time, he also felt a perverse resentment at her inner strength. Of how bravely she was making the choice to not let her father's betrayal ruin her.

He clearly didn't possess the same strength. He didn't have the generosity of spirit that she possessed. Even worse, he had no intention of for-giving anyone for anything.

Holding her like this, watching her choose joy and happiness over resentment and anger, he felt more than a little jaded. At twenty-nine, he felt as if he'd already lived through ten lifetimes of anger and resentment. All his choices in life now looked like they were tainted too.

Because he'd allowed the poison of his child-hood to run rampant inside him for his whole life.

"Thank you for listening to me, Dev," she said softly, pulling him back to the present. "For just about everything."

"I didn't do it for your gratitude, Clare."

"No, you did it because it was the right thing to do. Thanks to you, my faith in men isn't com-pletely dashed."

Dev shook his head. "Don't, Clare. This will benefit me too. So don't make me out to be some kind of hero." He pressed on. "But I know how hard it must have been to lay yourself open like that, so thank you for trusting me with the truth."

She looked up then, and the piercing quality of her gaze pinged through him. "I couldn't let you think I was that foolish anymore. It was fine when I thought you were just another only-in-it-for-a-good-time playboy."

He grinned at that. "I love these titles you keep coming up with for me."

"But none of them truly fit, do they?"

Dev frowned. "What do you mean?"

"I mean that I've seen more of the real you than you show the world, Dev. But there's still a lot more lying hidden. What was it you called it? Paying a toll? I don't want you to tell me as if it's a toll you're paying. I want you to want to tell me. I'd like to get to know the part of you that you don't show anyone else."

No one had ever asked him that. No one had ever cared enough to know. Not even his twin knew it all. But to confide in Clare meant something he wasn't prepared to admit to. "You're mistaking me for a deep lake. I'm a shallow pond, remember."

She pushed out of his arms and looked down at him. "All lies. But it's okay, Dev. If my pathetic excuse for a dad has taught me one thing, it's that you can't demand things from people—loyalty or love or even confidences—that they're unwilling to give. But I'd like you to know that I want more from you. From this partnership. More than orgasms, that is," she added candidly.

Dev had no idea how she did it—making demands of him he couldn't fulfill one minute and making him laugh the next. But there was no point in letting her think this was more than it was. His tone was grave when he said, "I've given you everything I'm capable of giving, Clare. Does that help?"

She scrunched her nose and smiled. A sad

smile. As if she understood even though he didn't say the words. "Not really. But I'll take that as a win for now. And now, I'm going to shower, eat a tub of ice cream and then your spare bed's got my name on it."

When she'd have slipped away, Dev pulled her back to him. He felt a strange reluctance to let her go, even though she'd be in the next room to his.

For the first time in his adult life, he felt an acute need for companionship. For more whispered confidences. For more of a connection with a woman than just a sexual one.

For all of those things with this particular woman.

And yet he didn't want to fight it. Or shove it away. Or call it a temporary madness.

In this moment, he felt all of that resentment and distance that forced him to stand alone in the world fall away. In this moment, he felt perfectly aligned with the universe and with Clare.

Her arms came around his neck as he pressed his mouth to the upper curve of her breast. He could taste the salt of the ocean, smell the sea breeze and her own distinct floral scent on her skin. Desire thrummed through him as she responded instantly. Her nails raked over his skin, and a shudder went through her.

Dev licked at the thundering pulse at her neck. He let his hands run rampant, caressing the dips and valleys of her body. He didn't even need this to go any deeper than it was right now. There was a sense of contentment in just holding her and in stoking the fire of their mutual desire higher and hotter.

With a muttered curse, she tugged his face to hers and kissed him fiercely.

Laughter and something else he didn't want to name held him in its grip as she devoured his mouth as if there was no end to her hunger for him. Dev had never been appreciated so thoroughly in his life.

When she let him go, he was rock hard, panting and desperate for more.

"Good night then," the minx whispered, a wicked glint in her blue eyes.

The dark shadows under her eyes tugged at him. "You don't have to go to bed alone tonight, Clare." When she smiled slowly, he held up his palm. "I'm not talking about sex. I'm concerned that nightmare you had on the yacht will be back."

"If it does, then you'll pick me up and bring me to your bed, won't you?"

She didn't wait for him to deny her. Not that Dev would have. He had a feeling he wouldn't have to share anything with her. Because the damned woman had seen and knew everything about him already.

More than he felt comfortable sharing with anyone.

"You're putting a lot of trust in me that's not warranted, Clare," he warned. "I'm no hero."

"Ha! Believe me, Dev, the last thing I need is a hero. Because they don't really exist, do they? If there is such a thing, it's people like us who live their lives, day after day, even though they've been dealt a bad hand."

"Then what is it you think you know about me, Clare?" he asked. He suddenly wanted her opinion. He wanted to know what it was that she thought of him.

"I think you're a man who wants more than he realizes. A man who doesn't have as much as he thinks he does. A man who has a lot more to give."

With that parting, perceptive shot, she walked away.

Making Dev wonder and question and doubt all the things he'd always thought were unshakeable truths about himself.

She was getting married in a few minutes.

As she looked at the knee-length, cream A-line dress she'd picked up during the short shopping jaunt that Dev had allowed her back in Rio before they'd spent several days sailing to his villa on St. Lucia, Clare wondered how many times she'd have to say it in her head for it sink in completely.

She was getting married to a man she would have preferred to like a little less than she did, even if that sounded more than a bit twisted. She was getting married without either of her best friends present. At the thought of Amy and Bea, her throat filled up.

The feel of the delicate silk under her fingers gave her something to anchor herself with, instead of focusing on the looping thoughts inside her head.

"He's really a catch, you know," Angelina Lansang continued her chatter without missing a beat. "Everyone that knows Dev is going to go crazy to discover he's secretly got hitched. The press, the media…" The tall woman laughed, a little bit inanely. As if this was the best thing about Dev getting married.

Do any of them actually know him? Clare wanted to ask. *Do they know that he's kind and far more complex than any interview or article could ever capture?*

But Clare didn't say anything of the sort, because sweet as Angelina had been during the time it had taken to sail to the island, she couldn't betray the fact that this was a fake wedding.

For a few, fleeting seconds, Angelina considered Clare thoughtfully before smiling again. "I hope you're ready for all the attention you're going to get, my dear." Clare resolutely kept her mouth closed.

* * *

Not only did she not know Angelina well enough, she didn't trust her own thoughts. Several days of pondering this every which way hadn't untangled her thoughts any better.

Since the other woman was waiting for a response, Clare smiled. "I can't thank you enough for everything, Angelina."

Angelina nodded, and returned her smile.

Ever since Clare and Dev had met up with Derek and Angelina the following day in Rio and he'd introduced Clare as his fiancée, asking them to join them at his villa and witness the ceremony, Angelina had completely changed her attitude. Not that Clare wasn't grateful.

It was, after all, thanks to Angelina's insistence that Dev had reluctantly agreed to Clare shopping for a suitable bridal outfit before leaving Rio. Not that Clare couldn't have fought that particular battle herself.

Even if the agreement between them was that this wedding was nothing but a mutually beneficial arrangement, she'd had no intention of marrying him wearing a trouser suit more suitable for business than pleasure.

Even if it was a designer suit.

It had been while they were having that discussion that Clare had finally lost the battle of pretending that this wedding mattered as little to her as it did to him.

Yes, this was a convenient arrangement that would benefit both of them. But it didn't mean that she couldn't feel some sentiment. That she could treat it as just any other normal day.

The wedding was only a technicality. She had silently recited that fact so often, it was as if it were her life's mantra. But looking at herself in the mirror, dressed as a bride, Clare knew no mantra was going to work on her.

Foolish or not, naive or not, she'd always dreamed of this day.

Because she was marrying Dev, Clare didn't even have to build her castles on the empty promises of a charming man who was all glitter and no substance. And it was this fact that kept tripping her up.

"You look beautiful." The surprise in Angelina's tone brought Clare back to the present.

She knew it didn't really matter how beautiful she looked. This marriage was only temporary and there would no doubt be countless other, far more beautiful women in Dev's life after she'd exited it. The thought darkened her mood, the pit of her stomach suddenly hollow. And that, in turn, flipped her mood back again. She was determined never to operate out of fear or loneliness ever again.

So what if she and Dev weren't going to promise to love each other for the rest of their lives? So what if their marriage came with a short shelf life?

She liked the man she was going to marry. She also very much liked what he was capable of doing to her with one playful glance from those twinkling eyes, with those clever fingers and with those sculpted lips. She wasn't going to pretend that she could be all matter-of-fact and cold about this. This was no fantasy she had concocted while waiting to escape from under the indifferent roof of her aunt.

This was her life.

Clare adjusted her hair and stared again at her reflection in the mirror. The dress was classy and elegant, but sexy enough as it clung to her curves. Her skillfully styled hair helped highlight her features. Her lipstick—a vibrant red—made her mouth look full and pouty.

She looked beautiful, she was getting married and she had the serious hots for her husband-to-be.

As she turned to leave the room, Clare told herself it was okay that this wedding felt real to her. It was the most real thing that had ever happened to her. And she was going to make the most of it.

"It's just a PR ploy," he'd said when his best friend had asked him what the hell he was playing at the night before his wedding.

"Like hell it is," Derek had said with a deep laugh. "You're in deep trouble, my man."

Now, as Dev watched his intended walk toward

him in his airy Caribbean villa, he felt Derek's words reverberate within his chest.

Clare looked nothing like some cheap participant in a PR ploy and everything like deep trouble poured into an enticingly petite frame. Just for him.

She looked stunning and elegant and beautiful in a cream-colored dress. Far too much like a real bride with her smile glowing and her eyes bright and generally radiating a serene kind of joy.

It reached Dev like a wave of emotion, intent on pulling him under.

He'd never given marriage much thought, except for knowing that it wasn't for him. He'd been far too busy building an empire.

But as he stood there, waiting for Clare to reach him, "PR ploy" felt like the most inadequate nonsense he'd ever uttered.

"You're in so much trouble, man," Derek whispered again with a pat on his shoulder.

Whatever retort he wanted to throw back at his friend died as Clare reached him. As he looked into the blue eyes of the woman he'd promised himself he'd look after. He hadn't, when he'd originally suggested the idea to her, thought to paint himself in the role of her hero.

For a long time, even into his adulthood, thinking himself as anything more than a failure had been hard. Even gaining Derek's friendship at military school and then discovering his talent for swimming, he'd struggled to see himself as anything but a disappointment to everyone around him.

Old patterns were hard to break.

It was only after he'd made his first million that Dev had felt a sense of achievement. Which was all kinds of messed up, he knew. Equating wealth and fame and power with self-worth was going down the same poisonous line of thinking Papa had employed when he'd scoured layers of Dev's self-esteem as a child with his harsh words.

You'll amount to nothing if you continue like this.

And the harshest cut of all: *Your mama's lucky to have gone before she saw you like this.*

By the time he'd realized that he'd started measuring himself by the same toxic yardstick as his father had done, it was too late to change. Plus, Dev had never been a hypocrite. He had enjoyed all the fame and wealth and power that his achievements and success had brought him.

Meeting Derek—who was six foot six and had weighed three hundred pounds as a sixteen-year-old, who was constantly viewed as a threat just because of his size and skin color while in actuality, the gentle giant possessed a heart of gold—had taught Dev a lot about how to manage people's perceptions.

So Dev knew there was a good reason Derek

was calling him on his nonsense about his marriage being a PR ploy.

But it *was* saving his reputation too, he reminded himself. This was letting up pressure on him, his family, his company and hopefully salvaging Athleta's reputation. They would both simply walk away from this in a few months with their problems solved. He hadn't told Clare yet, but he'd already had his security chief make contact with the mobster to start negotiations to try to pay off her debt.

This would be yet another satisfying business arrangement with a few pleasures thrown in as enjoyable extras. And he knew it wasn't just him thinking about sex.

But, as he glanced at the woman now standing beside him, Dev kept hearing Derek's sarcastic laughter inside his head.

Deep trouble, man...

It wasn't that her simple but stunning dress made her skin shimmer. It wasn't that she was holding a beautiful bouquet of lilies of the valley as a bride usually did. It wasn't even the platinum ring she'd produced in contrast to the plain gold band he'd selected at her suggestion.

It was the look in her blue eyes.

She didn't look at him as if this was a business arrangement. Or as if she was putting on an act. She simply looked as if she were gloriously happy to be marrying him. In that easy, let's-turn-Dev's-world-upside-down way that only she had.

From the first moment they'd met at that charity gala, she had seen him.

Him. Only him.

Dev Kohli. Not the shallow playboy, not the ruthless billionaire, not the *studly stud* as she'd called him, but just him.

It didn't matter that he hadn't given her what she'd asked for. It seemed as if she'd taken a part of him anyway, even without his permission.

As they stood there saying their vows, culminating with him bending his head and taking her mouth in a kiss that sealed her fate with his—at least temporarily—Dev had the uneasy feeling that he'd gone a step too far with this marriage. That he'd tangled himself into something he didn't quite understand.

Because no kiss had ever shaken him to his core like this one did.

Sweet and familiar, her lips molded to his in the exact way he needed them to. Her body pressed against his with that wide-open generosity of hers, her heart thudding against his own.

She felt like she belonged to him. In a way nothing and no one else ever had.

And, as he pulled away from her perceptive gaze, and laughed at some joke that Angelina cracked, his heart beating faster and faster, Dev wondered how he was going to fight it. How he was going to maintain any kind of distance when all he wanted was to steal her away for himself.

How he was going to walk away from her when all this was over.

CHAPTER TEN

"Are you drunk?"

Dev looked up from the open book in his lap he'd been flicking through for the last hour. The letters and words jumped and leaped on the page. Even more so than usual since his concentration was shot to hell.

He simply stared at Clare for a few seconds. Wondering if she was the cause or the means of escape from this torture.

She was standing with her back against the door to his bedroom. On the inside, he clarified for himself. The high walls and ceilings of his villa and all the skylights he'd had his architect install meant she was bathed in moonlight. Her freshly washed hair shone, and her eyes glittered with bright curiosity and something else as they swept over his naked chest.

Desire…and she didn't bother hiding it.

Awareness slammed through Dev.

She was his wife and he was her husband. He'd figured that a piece of paper with their signatures on it didn't really stand for much in the greater scheme of things. But he'd found that it did. He was discovering that maybe he was a traditional man at heart, after all.

A man who believed in marriage and family and all the things Mama had believed lay firmly at the center of human existence. But with that realization also came the acute feeling of inadequacy that he didn't like. It left a bad taste in his mouth. Reminded him of how he'd struggled with it for too many years. What if he wasn't any good as a husband?

This discovery about wanting things that he couldn't have, wouldn't be any good at, bothered him. After years of being a physically perfect championship-standard athlete and then his unprecedented success in the business world meant he'd forgotten how it felt to be bad at something. As a result, he was in a roaring bad mood. Which was really rare for him.

He shook his head. "No."

Arms folded against her chest, she rolled her eyes. "Good."

"What's good?" he asked, knowing that he was winding her up but enjoying it anyway. They were hitting that rhythm again. Bandying words while heat built around them. This was something he was exceptionally good at.

"Well, to start with, it's good that Derek and

Angelina seem to be getting through this rough patch," she said.

"Why is that good?"

"It's clear that you allow very few people into your life. Derek's happiness matters to you."

He grunted in response. Really, the last thing he wanted to talk about was Derek and Angelina's marriage. He didn't want to talk at all.

He wanted her. Desperately. He wanted to be inside her. He wanted to scratch this itch—as many times as required—and be done with it. He wanted to get rid of this sentimental nonsense that had taken over his head ever since he'd slipped the ring on her finger.

"You're not in a talking mood," she said, licking her lips.

"No."

"If anyone could see us now," she said, her eyes glinting with challenge, "they'd think I was the feudal lord and you my blushing bride."

He raised a brow. With each teasing word, she dispelled his dark mood. "And yet you're the one plastered to the door." He pushed the duvet down and patted the space next to him on the bed. "Care to try that theory by coming closer?"

Dev found his gaze eating her up, any remaining discontent washed away by curiosity and that simmering hum of desire.

"What the hell are you wearing?" he asked hoarsely.

She raised a rounded shoulder and one thin, almost nonexistent strap fell down. "This was the only thing I could find in the little time I had."

It was unlike anything Dev had ever seen, outside of maybe a period drama. It was all white and made of fine cotton. But without any ghastly ruffles.

The V-shaped bodice and the floaty hem that barely touched her knees stopped it from being plain. But, unlike silk that would have hugged her petite curves, this nightgown fluttered in the breeze through the open French doors, hinting at the dips and valleys of her body.

"You disappeared from dinner too soon," she said. "Those were your friends."

"I had things to look over."

"You don't have to run away from me, you know," she said. A hint of the fragility he'd sometimes seen in her peeked out from beneath the fierce scowl she wore.

"I've stopped running away from things that upset me a long time ago."

"So I'm one of those things, am I?"

He grinned. "If you were a thing I could put in a box so I could stop thinking about it, all of this would be easy. But you're not, are you? You're a…"

"What?"

He shrugged.

"I think the word you're looking for is *wife*.

With an independent mind and a beating heart and a…" She licked her lips and Dev felt a bolt of lust shoot through him. "I decided to let you be for a little while since you looked like you were upset."

He refused to answer.

Her lower lip trembled. "Regretting this already?"

"Not really," he said, loath to hurt her. "But you're right I'm not…in a good mood."

"Okay, that's fair enough," she said, that lost expression receding from her eyes. And Dev knew in that moment what was bothering him so much.

He didn't want to hurt her. He didn't want to be the reason the fierce light that was at the heart of Clare was diminished or even extinguished. He didn't want to be another man that made her think she was less than she was.

She wasn't that weak, he reminded herself. She'd understood what this arrangement of theirs meant. She'd accepted it.

And yet he couldn't shed this sense of responsibility he suddenly felt toward her. He turned the gold band on his finger, feeling the solid weight of the metal.

Her gaze flicked to the action and then up to his face. But her expression remained steady. And Dev knew he was just being unreasonable now.

"Do you want me to leave?" she asked.

* * *

It felt as if even the breeze and the world and time itself stood still to witness his answer. He rubbed a hand over his face. "No. I don't want you to leave, Clare."

She didn't quite smile. Her wide mouth softened.

"If I stay, I have some demands of you."

"Don't push it, sweetheart," he growled.

She laughed then. "If I stay, I'm going to want to exercise my marital rights. If you're not in the mood to accommodate me, or don't have the energy it requires, you should tell me now."

He burst out laughing, just as she'd intended. He licked his lower lip, sending a leisurely, thoroughly lascivious look up and down her body.

To his delight, pink crept up her neck and cheeks. "I'm always in the mood for you, Ms. Roberts," he said with a wicked grin.

She cocked an eyebrow. "You forget that I'm Mrs. Kohli now."

He fell back against the headboard. Warmth and something else suffused his chest. "That used to be Mama. I haven't heard that title in a long time."

Her fingers went to her chest and she bit her lip. "I'm sorry, Dev. I didn't mean to poke fun at it."

"Don't be," Dev said. This time, the mention of his mother didn't leave a painful void in its wake. Not here, with the only other woman who saw through his surface qualities. Who'd always looked at him as if he could be more. As if he was more. More than the world thought him to be. More than he thought himself to be. "I have a feeling she'd have liked you."

Clare's smile put the moonlight to shame. "You think so?"

Dev nodded, feeling a sudden stab of such overpowering grief mixed in with this new feeling of joy. "Yes. She'd have especially liked how often you keep me on my toes."

She smiled. "You miss her a lot."

He shrugged. "Yes, each year, I miss her more."

"She sounds like a wonderful woman."

"She was. She…had the knack of seeing through to a person's heart. And finding something to love in everyone."

"Will you tell me more about her?"

His chest rose and fell as Dev considered this woman…his wife. She always wanted more. More of life. More of herself. More of him. "I will. But some other time. Not tonight." He beckoned her closer. "Tonight is about you and me, Clare. Only you and me." Now that he'd made peace with that fact, the slumbering need in him had risen keenly to the surface.

Why had he even been fighting this so much?

She blushed prettily, even as she demanded

he give her what she wanted. "I have a wedding present for you."

Dev felt like he had been knocked over the head. Although he didn't know why he should be so surprised. She'd already told him that she wasn't going to pretend this was a cold, dry business arrangement.

"I have nothing for you."

She clearly wasn't disappointed by that. "I didn't expect you to get me anything. I saw this when I went shopping with Angelina and it made me think of you. Don't worry, Dev. I know what I want from you."

He raised a brow, unashamedly eating her alive with his eyes. He could see the shadow of her nipples through the nightgown, the slightly rounded shape of her belly when it was plastered to her body by the friendly breeze, and a darker shadow at the apex of her thighs. "I should tell you, Clare, that I don't have either the patience or the inclination to be overly gentle tonight."

She swallowed and he saw the flutter of her pulse at her neck. "I never asked you to be gentle with me. It's your own fault if you catered to me. But then, that's what you do, don't you?"

He frowned. "I have no idea what you mean."

"That night, I didn't ask you to be gentle with me. I didn't tell you that it was my first time. It was what I needed and you simply gave it to me. That's who you are, Dev. Why fight it?"

"And here I thought you dwelled in reality, Clare."

She was hurt by that. He'd only meant to pierce the false image of him she was building in her head. Because he sure as hell couldn't be that man.

But instead of backing down, she covered the distance between them. Now she stood close enough that he could smell the lily of the valley on her. The taut buds of her nipples taunted him. "We all need a dose of cold reality most days, I agree. But as I realized recently, a little dreaming never hurt anyone. In fact, it was the thing that sustained me through so many difficult years."

When he opened his mouth, she pressed her palm to his lips. "It's okay. I don't want to argue tonight. I have other plans—devious plans," she said with a naughty grin.

Lust kicked through him. "I should very much like to be part of your plans, Clare."

In one easy movement, he picked her up and brought her onto the bed. She landed on her knees, on the duvet, his legs still buried beneath it. The scent of her skin enveloped him and he breathed it in, like a junkie.

He took the square package with the neat bow and was about to toss it aside when she grabbed it and held it up to him.

"So that's how it's going to be, huh?" he said, burying his face in her neck. The uproar that had begun in his chest hours earlier calmed at the feel of her soft curves in his hands.

"I want you, Dev. I want to spend tonight with you. More than anything in the world. But…"

He pulled back and smiled. "Okay. I guess it's true what they say about marriage, huh?"

Her eyes widened and she played along. The twitch of her mouth made his heart swell in his chest. "What do they say about marriage, Dev?"

"That the sex dries up and your wife rules you."

"Hey," she said, swatting him on the shoulder.

Dev took the wrapped package from her hands. "All right, fine. If this is what it takes…"

Her teeth digging into her lower lip, she looked at him from under her lashes.

Curiosity took over and he ripped the wrapping off.

To find a cardboard box in his hand—an audiobook of an autobiography of a black American athlete who'd found success despite numerous obstacles. Dev had been sent an autographed copy by the gentleman. It was the one book he didn't have in audio.

So of course, he hadn't read it.

Dev stared at it for what felt like interminable seconds, alarm coursing down his spine. Tension burst into life around them, replacing all the desire and humor that he'd felt so drunk on.

He looked up to find Clare watching him.

He had no idea what she saw in his face. A nervous laugh escaped her mouth. "I noticed that you don't have the audiobook for this title."

"When?" he said. Because he had to say something to cut the awkwardness. Because to say nothing at all would betray his shock.

"Oh, I told you, I loved that library of yours. It's so well categorized that it wasn't hard to see that this one was missing."

"Yeah, I meant to get it."

"Are you angry, Dev?" Her mouth was pinched, her eyes wide. "I didn't do it to pry. Like I said, that library…it was like a part of you. I thought I…"

"No, you aren't prying," he said, stunned by how perceptive she was. He rubbed a hand over his face. "And I'm not angry." But there was something in his tone that even he couldn't identify.

Was it still just shock that had him struggling to form thoughts and sentences? Only Derek knew. It had been him who'd insisted that Dev get diagnosed. That it wasn't too late. Never too late. And of course the therapist that Dev had gone to after he'd been diagnosed knew. Not even Diya had guessed or asked.

"It's not something I ever discuss," he said, his voice hoarse. "If I'd had the diagnosis of dyslexia as a child, then it might have been different."

If he thought she'd nod and agree and close the subject, he was wrong.

Clare frowned, her palms on his bare shoulders, grounding him.

"In fact, your success, your company…you're the symbol of what one can accomplish despite being wired differently."

"Before you ask, no, I'm not ashamed of being dyslexic, Clare."

He felt that maybe he should have moderated his curt tone, but right now, the last thing he felt like doing was pacifying her or anybody else for that matter. He had always struggled alone in his life. Nothing was ever going to change that.

"I didn't think you were, Dev."

"I wasn't diagnosed until very late. Not until I was seventeen."

"But you come from such an affluent, educated family."

He laughed then, and it was the hollowest sound he'd ever heard. "You want the whole sorry story then?"

She nodded, still touching him. Still anchoring him.

"I was a very…rambunctious kid. As Deedi tells it—that's my older sister—I was slow to speak. My mother apparently schlepped me around to a lot of speech therapists. So it was decided at a very early age that of the four of us, I wasn't the brightest bulb."

"Who decided that?" Clare asked with such a fierce scowl that Dev rubbed his fingers against her brow.

"My father. But Mama wouldn't listen to him. She tried her best to help me sit down and focus. And I tried. For her, I tried so hard. But letters and words were nothing but a jumble to me. The more I tried to pin them down, the more they escaped me.

"So I started cutting classes. I started paying a friend to do my work for me. I manipulated Diya into doing my homework. I cheated as much as I could. Anything and everything to not disappoint Mama. Anything to avoid telling her the truth. Because the one thing I couldn't do was bring myself to admit that I just couldn't read. That all the books she bought me…she might as well have asked me to walk to the moon.

"After a while, all my schemes were found out. Diya got into big trouble. My friend was forever banished from seeing me. I begged Papa to not have him expelled from school. That it was all my fault. That I had manipulated them all into helping me. Mama was crushed. I've never felt as low as I did that day when she realized I'd been cheating when she'd thought I'd been getting better."

"Oh, Dev. I'm so sorry."

"I hadn't wanted to disappoint her. And I ended up crushing her. Betraying her faith in me."

"Then?"

It felt as if there were shards stuck in his throat. "She still tried. I got expelled from three different private schools for getting into trouble. She tried private tutoring and every other option out there. I'd hear them arguing at night. Hear him call me useless and stupid and her fighting with him to not call her baby boy that. Arguing that academic success wasn't everything. That she'd spend her life helping me if that's what it took. Papa was furious with me. I think more than that, it scared him. He couldn't see why one of his children wasn't like the other three. He couldn't fathom that his son was such a loser. That I resented him and argued with him and gave him attitude at every turn didn't help our relationship, either."

"But you were a kid, Dev. Just a kid. We shouldn't have to make allowances for adults and their feelings." Dev held her, hearing the pain he'd once felt echoing in her voice.

"Please tell me he didn't abuse you to your face," Clare whispered against his shoulder. "Please tell me your mother stopped him."

Dev shook his head. "He didn't call me a dumb loser, no. That was one of the names I called myself. He called me lazy, incompetent. A rogue who didn't appreciate the privileges he had. A boy who was good for nothing. Then when I was twelve, Mama died."

Clare's arms were around his neck now, her own trembling.

Dev pressed his palms to her back, glad to have her here. "The worst part is over, sweetheart."

She pulled back and glared at him. "How can you be so cavalier about this, Dev?"

"Because I can't let it be more, Clare. It's taken me years to not think of myself as a failure. Hours of therapy to realize that my brain's just wired differently. That not being able to read—something my mother loved to do with me—didn't mean the world of books wasn't cut off for me. Whenever I thought about the past, I had to develop a degree of emotional separation from it. Or I'd have ruined my life with my own hands."

"What did your father do then? After she died."

"He packed me off to military school barely a week later. Diya told me Deedi and Bhai had a huge fight with him about it, but he wouldn't listen to anyone. His grief found an outlet in me, I think. And I was happy to leave a place that no longer held the one person who'd loved me unconditionally."

"You haven't been back there since, have you?"

Dev looked into her eyes and shook his head. "No. And the thought of going back now is painful. But for Diya... I have to."

"How was the military school?"

"In retrospect, it was the best place for me. It was rigorous and disciplined and when night came, I was simply too exhausted to think of my shortcomings. I met Derek there. And one of the coaches found something to nurture in the both of us. The rest is history."

"You're a testament to—"

Dev pressed his finger to her lips. "I don't want praise, sweetheart."

She nodded, and he smiled. "I want the wedding night that I was promised. No, that you demanded that I give you. I want you to look at me as you always do."

"You think hearing this has changed how I see you?" she asked with a frown.

"Does it?"

"Of course not, you arrogant man. It only makes me want to jump your bones even more. There, is that what you want to hear?"

"Yes," Dev said, before dipping his mouth to hers.

It shouldn't have made a difference that she knew about his childhood. About the difficulties he'd had to overcome. Some he still lived with to this day.

But as Dev swept his tongue into her welcoming mouth, as he filled his hungry hands with her curves and kissed her harder and deeper, he felt as if for the first time in his life, someone knew who he was. What he'd achieved to get here. He felt...whole. Even though he hadn't realized what he'd been missing.

Hands wrapping around her slender shoulders, he gathered her closer to him.

"Yes, please. God, yes, Dev. Now," she replied. The throaty need in her voice undid Dev just a little bit more.

The taste of her skin under his tongue felt like peace and joy and contentment like he had never known before.

She was trembling as he nipped and kissed his way from her neck to the soft, silky smooth skin of her jaw. He couldn't touch her enough. Couldn't taste her enough. He licked the delicate lobe of her ear.

She shuddered, a long moan rasping out of her throat and pressed herself against him. Her breasts crushed against his chest, her lips sought his. Dev devoured her mouth as if he was a drowning man. As if the taste of her could bring him back to shuddering life from the cold, sterile reality he'd existed in for so many years.

Suddenly his life before she'd come barging into it felt…flat, one-dimensional. A glittering mockery of the real thing.

Dev had no idea who pushed the duvet out from between them. He had no idea if he was the one who pulled up the flimsy little thing that she was wearing and threw it off. He didn't know if she demanded, or he had created a space between his thighs for her.

But as their frenzied kiss deepened, he filled

his hands with the slight weight of her breasts. She straddled his hips, moving up and over him, until she was exactly where she wanted to be.

He nipped her lower lip when she rubbed herself against his hardness, and then flicked his tongue over it. Her fingers sneaked into his hair and tugged imperiously.

"Inside me, now, Dev," she whispered frantically.

He suddenly hesitated.

She moved his head so she could see into his eyes, her own feverish with desire. "You said you had no inclination to be slow or gentle tonight. I find that I'm desperate for hard and fast tonight. So how about you make good on your promise?"

Filling his hands with her slender hips, Dev lifted her up. She moaned as he lowered his thumb to her core. Slowly, he drew it down, down, down until his thumb was notched at the entrance of her sex. Her dampness drenched him. His erection lengthened further as she wound herself around him like a vine, thrusting her pelvis into his hand.

"I love how greedy you are, sweetheart," he whispered, dipping his finger in and out of her, feeling anticipation bunch his muscles rock hard.

"You make me like this. Only you," she whispered, her face buried in his shoulder.

Dev took another few seconds teasing her out, though it felt like an eternity. With his other palm, he stroked the warm, damp planes of her body. Rubbed the tight knot of her nipple between his fingers. Up on her knees, she thrust into his hand with a frantic urgency that made his throat dry.

Her eyes closed, her neck thrown back, she was lost in sensation. "Do you like this?" he growled, wanting to hear her voice.

"Faster, Dev. Damn it, give me what I want. Please."

He laughed, and she opened those blue eyes and bent to kiss him. Hard and rough, winding him up even more.

"I love it when you laugh," she said, and Dev felt like he was drenched in her shy smile.

He flicked at her sensitive bud gently and felt her responsive shudder. She moved forward and back, her breasts rubbing against his chest, pleasure painting her face a lovely pink. He tormented her for little while more, loving her moans and whispers that told him she was getting closer to ecstasy.

Just when she was hovering right on the edge of the abyss, he pulled back to quickly sheathe himself.

Lifting her with one hand on her buttock, Dev took his shaft in the other and slowly, carefully, slid himself inside her soft, wet heat.

She was incredibly snug around him, and he thought he might have died a little with sheer pleasure.

Her long, guttural moan mingled with his.

Her blue eyes deepened into a darker color, glittering with raw pleasure. She brought his palm to her left breast and sighed.

Dev kneaded her breast obediently, the tip of her nipple pressing into his palm. He didn't move his hips for long minutes. He didn't want to move, even though his body was screaming for release. He intended to savor this moment.

He kissed her brow and tasted the dampness from her skin.

Her gaze held his, shining so brightly that Dev wanted to look away.

But he forced himself to hold it. To see this woman who was a fighter just like him.

"You feel like you're inside me, all the way to here," she moaned, and then she threw her arms around his neck and held him tight.

Dev started to build their pace with slow, deep thrusts. He had a feeling he was never going to get enough of her. That one fine morning, he was going to wake up to find she'd changed him forever.

She matched his rhythm perfectly, bearing down when he thrust up, meeting him stroke for stroke. He glided his palms all over her silky back, following the curve of her hips, and chasing a drop of sweat trailing down her cleavage, before moving to take the begging tip of her dark pink nipple into his mouth. He bit back a groan as she shuddered as she approached her own peak.

And when she was close again, this time he pushed her over the edge with his fingers.

She orgasmed with a low cry, her nails clutching his shoulders, marking him. And in the hold and release of her climax, Dev chased his own.

With one swift movement, he turned her back against the sheets, and then he lost himself in the arms of his wife.

CHAPTER ELEVEN

THE KOHLIS' HOUSE in California was really a mansion. Even knowing that this trip was mostly about Dev and not her—which meant she was hoping she wouldn't be under too much scrutiny from his big family—Clare couldn't help being nervous.

Fake marriages were not easy. Especially when you were married to a gorgeous hunk with kind eyes and complex emotional depths. Especially when she and Dev made it all too real when it came to passion. Especially when during the two weeks since their wedding, she'd seen how much they had in common.

She tried to bury her anxiety by telling herself that he needed her to be confident and charming and perfect. Not because she needed to impress anyone in particular. But because that was the only way his family would believe that he'd fallen for her.

She *was* all of those things, she reminded herself. The only playacting that they needed to engage in was convincing everyone that they were hopelessly in love with each other. That was the part she was looking forward to.

She couldn't wait to see how Dev was going to pull it off.

Tall Oaks stood in solemn welcome, straddling a wide pathway with lush, green vegetation on each side for almost a few kilometers before they arrived at the residence.

By this time, Clare was used to the grandeur and affluence that followed Dev wherever he went. But as she stepped out of the chauffeured Mercedes and stared up at marble facade of the gigantic mansion, Clare wasn't quite as composed as she'd have liked to have been.

A lump filled her throat.

She couldn't stop imagining Dev here as a little boy. Rambunctious and full of energy, yet confused by his incapability to understand the written word. Being surrounded by a genius brother and overachieving sisters, while letters and words escaped him.

And when he'd finally begun to realize that there might be a reason for that, he'd already lost his champion—his mother.

Tears filled her eyes as she recalled what he'd told her about his father's treatment of him, and Clare blinked them back. She could imagine him here, running wild, losing himself in the woods.

Trying to free himself from the stifling expectations and his own shortcomings.

Feeling like he could breathe again.

She sent him a sideways glance, knowing he'd hate to be pitied. But Clare had always known herself. Had always faced her truths.

What she felt for Dev wasn't pity at all.

She reached out and took his hand in hers. He was stiff at first, his jaw tightly locked. But slowly, he tangled his long fingers with hers and his breath came out in a long, painful exhale.

He met her gaze only once. But it was enough for Clare. It was more than enough.

He knew she was here, in this moment with him. He knew he wasn't alone. And with that one glance, he acknowledged it. It told her that her presence did make a difference to him.

Clare knew he couldn't give her any more than that. Knew that he might never look any deeper at what their marriage had morphed into. Knew that she might have to wait a long time, maybe even forever, to hear what he felt for her.

But she didn't care.

She was happy to be here and share this moment with him.

She was relieved to find that her father's betrayal hadn't put her off forging new connections with people.

She was also ecstatic and a little terrified that

she might be falling in love with her commitment-phobic husband whose scars ran so deep.

"So how did you and my brother meet?"

Clare looked up from the intricate swirls the henna artist was drawing on her left palm with a dexterity that left her in awe of her talent.

To find about twenty sets of eyes on her.

Her heart beat to the rhythm of the Bollywood Hip Hop fusion music that was blaring out from cleverly hidden speakers in the backyard. Despite the noise, it felt as if everyone and everything around her had fallen silent just to hear her answer.

And there was a lot going on.

Whatever she had read previously about Indian weddings, Clare had discovered that the reality gloriously outmatched the theory. It wasn't just people dressed in beautiful clothes, long-lost cousins greeting each other, kids from old family friends eyeing each other now that they were grown up, interfering aunties sizing up brides for their sons and vice versa, it was the sheer joy that pervaded the atmosphere. Diya had laughed and told Clare that by marrying Dev she'd apparently saved him from a huge peril in the form of a pushy auntie who wanted to matchmake for him.

It was also the ceremony after ceremony of teasing the bride and the groom, of dancing and food, of being a part of something that was much bigger than yourself.

Oh, Clare knew there were bound to be downsides too, but she didn't care. Not when smiling aunties and uncles she didn't know looked her up and down, kissed her cheek and demanded she—Dev's lovely new bride—take their blessings for a long, prosperous marriage.

It had taken a giggling Diya to explain that in this context, prosperity was all the children she and Dev might have in the future.

And at the thought of children—her and Dev's children—of a boy or a girl with their father's twinkling eyes, his beautiful jet-black hair, and that sheer determination to conquer life, Clare had known it was too late for her.

She badly wanted this marriage to be a real one. She wanted that future with Dev. She wanted…so much she knew she couldn't have.

Ever since they'd arrived here, he'd changed. Oh, he'd laughed and joked with people, played the doting uncle to a number of nieces and nephews, chatted with Diya for a bit, sitting in the lighted courtyard while the groom, Richard, and Clare had waited patiently.

There was a sadness in him, Clare could tell. If he had expected to feel different returning here as a successful businessman, as a world-renowned billionaire, she knew he had failed.

She saw it in his eyes.

She felt it in the silence he imposed between them at night when she crawled into bed after a long day of festivities. When he reached for her and made love to her with a dark passion, as if he needed escape.

Clare loved sleeping next to his large, warm body. Loved it when he cuddled her body against his, whispering soft endearments in her ear.

But it was clear that being back in his childhood home had cast a darkening spell on him. Clare knew that his twin looked at him with concern. But he'd shrugged her concern away in front of Clare. Had then evaded a more in-depth conversation with Clare as if he didn't trust his own words.

As if he could only communicate with his mouth and his fingers and his body.

So Clare let him. She let him take whatever he needed from her. Because she loved him with all her heart.

She finally knew it for certain when she washed off her hennaed hand and saw that the artist had inserted Dev's name so cleverly into the swirls on Clare's palm.

She rubbed at his name with her finger and took a deep, shaking breath.

Knew that he'd carved himself into her heart too.

Whatever she told herself, or however well she prepared herself for the worst didn't matter.

She'd fallen in love with Dev Kohli, and there was nothing she could do about it. Most of the time, Clare didn't want to. Because loving him meant being her best self. Seeing herself through his eyes. Seeing the very fabric and future of her life shift with him in it.

God, she wanted him in it so desperately.

"Clare?"

She looked up to see Dev's older sister—and everyone else—still waiting for an answer as to how they'd met. "Sorry, I drifted off there for a moment!" She strained her brain trying to think of the right story to tell while the artist took hold of her other hand.

She spotted the tall figure of Dev's dad hulking against the back wall, listening. to whom apparently, appearances were everything.

When Dev had first introduced her to Anand Kohli, he had greeted Clare with a warmth she hadn't expected. And when she'd trotted out her qualifications as the CEO of her own company, approval had glinted in the brown eyes that were so much like Dev's.

But the similarities had ended there. The older man didn't appear to have the warmth her husband did. Neither did he seem to possess the kindness and generosity of spirit that was so much a part of Dev's personality.

A tall, broad man like his son, he had retained

his good looks and stature. Clare had tried to imagine him angry and impatient with a little boy who couldn't put his troubles into words. As a hard man who demanded perfection instead of seeing the lonely, lost child.

Clare had never felt an anger before like she had felt it then, on behalf of that young Dev.

In a booming voice, he'd prodded Dev about not informing his family about his nuptials.

And Dev had simply shrugged. Refusing to pretend as if everything was normal between them. As if he had any obligation to his father. He's simply walked away, leaving them both staring after his retreating back.

Clare had automatically turned to apologize to the older man for Dev's behavior but managed to swallow it. This man didn't deserve an apology. Not when he was responsible for all the scars that Dev bore.

And yet…as she'd stood there facing him, she'd thought of her own father. Of how angry she'd have been if she had ever laid eyes on him again. How she'd have demanded an explanation for what he'd done.

How, if he'd offered even a tiny excuse, she'd have tried to forgive him. Would he have been genuinely sorry was a question she was never going to get answered.

But Dev's father was here. Alive. Despite everything, there was something about him that had made her feel sorry for him too.

"He likes you," Mr. Kohli had said then, a hint of shock in his voice. Whatever flash of raw ache she'd seen in his eyes gone now.

Her hackles had risen. "The last thing you should be doing now, Mr. Kohli, is criticizing your son's choice of wife."

He'd smiled then, as if he was some maharaja granting a boon to a peon. "Oh, I wasn't criticizing his choice, Clare. I was surprised, that's all."

"By what?" she'd demanded, more curious than angry now.

"I never thought he'd marry. But not only did he tie the knot, he seems to have traveled a different route to it than I or any of his siblings expected him to."

"Again, I'm not sure if you're insulting me or complimenting me."

His gaze dwelled thoughtfully on where Dev had stood not a minute ago. "After all the women that have paraded through his life, I'm glad he's chosen a wife that suits him so well. The real him. His mother would've been happy to see you with him."

Clare had been struck mute that father and son would think the same thing. "Why do you say that?" she'd asked, fishing for more.

Mr. Kohli's dark eyebrows had tied together.

"It's clear that he's happy with you. Even though he thinks I don't know him."

"But you don't," Clare had whispered. She'd walked away then, without waiting for his reply.

"Clare?"

Diya's hand on her arm brought Clare back to the present once again. She forced a deep breath in and smiled. Lies were easier if they were mostly truth embroidered, weren't they? Not that she'd ever come back here and see these lovely faces again.

"Oh, I…snuck onto Dev's yacht," she said with a dramatic roll of her eyes.

A barrage of whoops and questions came back at her.

She laughed. "I had one date with him and after that he blew me off. So when I had the chance to attend a party aboard his yacht, I crept into his bedroom. And demanded that he—"

"She demanded that I either give us another chance or toss her overboard," an amused voice finished behind her.

Clare tilted her head back to find Dev looking down at her from his great height. He was wearing a half-white kurta with gold piping across the Nehru collar, and he looked gorgeous in a more subdued than usual kind of way.

Laughter and cheers surrounded them. More questions came, but Clare couldn't look away from his dark gaze. She must have moved her other hand to keep her balance because the henna artist was suddenly muttering away in Hindi.

Her heart thumped wildly as Dev fell to his knees behind her. His arm came around her waist, taking her weight and keeping her hand steady for the artist. And then he was dipping his head—uncaring of all the eyes watching—and kissing her.

More squeals abounded them, a deafening jumble of catcalls and whistles, and Clare thought she might cry at the tenderness with which he kissed her. Softly, slowly, almost reverently.

As if he were seeking a benediction. As if he were asking for something he couldn't put into words.

Clare wrapped her free hand around his neck and held on. Her heart racing so fiercely that she thought it might pound right out of her chest.

It had been like this ever since their wedding night. One kiss led to more. A hundred kisses led to everything. Everything led to her being suffused by emotions for this man.

His fingers held her jaw for his tongue's foray now. If he weren't holding her steady, Clare knew she'd have melted right onto the marble floor. She sighed when he finally let her go.

"What was that for?" she asked, rubbing her fingers tentatively over her swollen lips.

He jerked his chin back for a second. As if he found the question unexpectedly daunting. As if he couldn't think of the right words. Something shifted in his gaze and then he said, "Did I tell you how lovely you look in your lehenga?" he said, a smooth charm back in his voice.

Disappointment flooded Clare. Not that she believed his compliment to be false; the traditional outfit Diya had presented her with was gorgeous, with gold embroidery enhancing the stunning pale pink color. But because he had pushed away whatever it was that had tugged him to her in this moment. Whatever he'd been silently telling her with that kiss was now neatly forgotten again.

"Thank you," she said inanely. "How did the male bonding go last night?"

He grinned. "It was boring… Bhai doesn't drink. Richard is quiet. Then Derek showed up and it felt like a party."

"Did you and your brother get a chance to talk?" she asked, knowing that Dev had been evading his brother too.

A shutter fell over his expression. "Let it go, Clare."

Clare refused to indulge in the hurt that splintered through her. This wasn't about her. This was about him.

"I came to see if they were bothering you," he said in a loud whisper that was intended to reach his sisters.

Clare leaned back against his broad frame,

feeling as if she was being torn between joy and a searing longing for more.

"Oh…pshh…your bride is safe with us," Diya answered her brother, while most of the crowd turned back to the business at hand. And then she dipped her head and planted a kiss on Clare's cheek.

Dev stared at his twin, while Clare felt as if she'd just been given a wonderful gift. She clutched Diya's hand, a prickle of tears in her throat. "What was that for?"

Diya grinned, and her eyes were glittering bright with their own wetness. "Just for coming into his life. He… I haven't seen him like this in a long time. A very long time."

Before Dev or Clare could stay her, Diya walked away, leaving a sudden silence behind.

Clare would've given anything, anything in the world, to have Dev acknowledge what his twin had just said.

She willed him with everything in her to say one word. Something. Anything.

Time ticked away, seconds to minutes, leaving her desperately aching.

She shivered, the chill coming from inside her rather than out. His body was there instantly, warm and hard. She felt his chin touch her head, his kiss at her temple. But this time, Clare wanted the words. Needed them like she needed air to breathe.

She was just beginning to think she was going to have to wait forever again. Just as she'd waited for her father...months upon months, melting away into years after years. Believing. Hoping. Sustaining herself for so long on so very little.

His hands stayed around her waist. "I have something for you."

"My wedding present?" she said, asking the same question for the hundredth time.

It had started as a joke between them. A game. But now, as his gaze met hers and held it, it became something more. Something portentous.

"No," he said, shaking his head. "Even better."

Clare pouted playfully. "Tell me."

"My security team has been in negotiations with the mobster. He's finally agreed to let me..." He trailed off then, looking slightly uneasy for a moment.

"Let you what?" she asked suspiciously.

"Let me buy you off him."

"The absolute gall of the man!" she erupted. "I'm not a camel!"

Taking her chin in his hand, Dev bent and dropped a brief kiss on her lips. "I know, sweetheart. But you're forgetting the bright spot in all this. You'll be free, Clare, very soon. You'll never have to be afraid of anyone again. Ever."

Clare threw her arms around him. He held her

through the shiver that went through her at the realization she was finally free. "Thank you," she whispered.

When he let her go and stood up, she couldn't help saying, "But that pushes us one step closer, doesn't it?"

"To what?" he asked, looking confused.

"To dissolving this...arrangement. Once we've sorted out your reputation too, we can be done with each other. And as there are already lots of positive stories in the world's media about your wedding, as well as the interviews we've done with Ms. Jones and your sisters, I'd say we're nearly there already."

For once, Clare didn't wait to see what he would say. She didn't think she could bear it if he simply agreed with her. Or made a joke of it.

So she carefully held the hem of her gorgeous pink skirt with one hand and walked away, wondering why she was feeling so odd when she was on the cusp of having her freedom again.

She'd never wanted more in her life to be called back. Never wanted to hear her name on his lips so badly.

She didn't even have to give up her company. Yes, she'd pay Dev back what he'd had to pay the mobster, even if it took her years to do it, but it wasn't a deadly sword hanging over her head any longer.

Yet, instead of elation, all she felt was desolation.

As if she'd been left all alone in the world again.

CHAPTER TWELVE

"ARE YOU GOING to talk to him?"

Dev had known this was coming. He'd seen the combative look in Clare's eyes over the last three days. He knew all her looks now.

Her "I'm ready for battle" look.

Her "I want you so I'm going to have you" look.

Her "Do you really want to try me?" look.

And Dev adored them all. But this look indicating that she was going to prod and push, he disliked with a vengeance.

Her chin tilted high, her wide mouth pursed in dissatisfaction; she'd been retreating from him ever since he'd told her that she was going to be free of the crime lord. Irritation flickered through him. He hadn't expected her to fall on him in gratitude but he had expected… What?

She'd reminded them both of their agreement. That they were getting much closer to being able to end this charade. It was a reminder he'd desperately needed.

A reminder he shouldn't have needed, given how busy they'd been continuing to make his halo shine.

They hadn't been free for even one evening.

If it wasn't some wedding ceremony that Diya insisted they both join, it was attending a charity auction where Clare had trumpeted to the media about the annual charity retreat Athleta held with star athletes. Another afternoon had been spent at an inner-city youth hostel that Dev had always supported financially.

Derek and Angelina had been there at the hostel, all their issues resolved. Although he was pleased for his friend, something about how in tune they'd been had grated at Dev, amplifying the disconnect between him and Clare.

They had spent a perfect California afternoon—Derek and he playing flag football with the teens while Clare and Angelina spent more than two hours in conversation with the warden and the press that Clare had invited.

If he wasn't so wrapped up in his own thoughts, Dev would have laughed at how dictatorial his wife could get when she was on a schedule. How dedicated she was to her job of making him look good.

How easily she'd weaved herself into his life. Into his family's affections.

He'd seen his brother—who was even more allergic to having heart-to-hearts than Dev was—

have a long, involved talk with her. He'd even seen his father voluntarily strike up conversations with her. Not that it was a big leap to find Clare interesting.

He'd seen Diya and his older sister with her—their heads bent together, laughing at one joke or another. And then Clare would look up—as if she had some kind of sensor for locating him—and they would stare at each other across the room, that ever-present desire shimmering like an arc between them, connecting them.

He would normally have winked and smiled at her, and she'd have blushed. Whatever the time of the day. Wherever they were.

Except she'd stopped smiling and blushing at him during the last three days. She didn't chatter away asking about this aunt who'd run away with her girlfriend twenty years ago creating a huge scandal or that uncle who'd maintained two families for years. She had retreated from him.

Each night, Dev had crawled into bed, expecting to be given the cold shoulder there too. Dreading it, in fact. Because he wasn't sure he could stand if she turned away from him there as well. Not just because he wanted to make love to her again. That desire for her was always there. He'd made peace with that.

But because those nights with her had become his escape from the grief he still felt being back here, in his family home. From the pain of feeling like a stranger among his own family.

Holding her, kissing her, making love to her had become the anchor he needed to shore up his days.

But to his shock and unending relief, her slender body had pressed up against his. Her palm on his chest, she'd burrowed into him.

She'd done it again last night too. The soft warmth of her body had instantly set him on edge.

"Clare, what's—"

She had pressed her palm over his mouth and shook her head. "I don't want to talk, Dev. Please, will you just…make love to me?"

"Yes," he had whispered, taking the easy way out.

Then she'd pulled him on top of her. The dark night had swallowed up his ragged moan as he entered her in one deep thrust. The breeze buried her gasp as he took her with a desire that didn't abate until he'd driven them both to a glorious release.

And when he'd found her cheek damp afterward, Dev had simply held her while her breathing slowly returned to normal. While she slipped into sleep. But he had stayed awake. Thinking.

He had no idea what the hell he was expecting from her or himself. They weren't, after all, truly married.

"Are you just going to pretend that I'm not standing here haranguing you?" she demanded now, interrupting his thoughts.

"You sound like a proper fishwife, sweetheart," Dev said, determined to make her smile today. He looked up and his own smile disappeared. He felt as if he'd been kicked in the stomach. Hard.

Today, she was wearing a light blue kurta that made her beautiful eyes pop, with a wide round neck and flared pants. A tiny red bindi between her eyebrows sent shock waves through him.

Eyes wide, he stared at the delicate black bead necklace at her throat with a diamond at the center.

His fingers were shaking when he pushed his hair back. "What—" he had to clear her throat "—what are you wearing? I thought all the ceremonies were finished last night."

A wariness entered her eyes, and she touched her fingers to her throat. "They are. Diya and Richard are leaving for Malibu in two hours. This…your aunts and Deedi and Diya…they had a small ceremony for me first thing this morning."

"What?" he barked.

But she didn't back down. "Since we cheated them out of attending our wedding, they sprang a surprise celebration for me. To welcome me as the daughter-in-law of the house. Your father was there too. They all gave me presents—jewelry, clothes. And this…" she said, touching that necklace again.

"It belonged to my mother."

"I know. Diya told me. I told her I couldn't just take it like that. They didn't listen. She kept saying your mother would've wanted me to have it. That she'd have been overjoyed if she'd been here today."

Dev looked away, feeling as if his heart had crawled up into his throat. "Of course."

"You don't have to be upset about this," Clare said to his back, her voice all matter-of-fact. He wondered if she could sense the chaotic mess his heart was in. If she could see how much he wanted her to have it. How much…he was struggling with that want.

He wanted to let this thing between them grow into what it had the potential to be. He wanted to lean into it with all his being and yet…something stopped him. Something always held him back.

Being here, in his childhood home, didn't help.

"I'm not planning to steal it, Dev. I figured it was easier to go along with what they wanted and then just return it to you afterward. Unless you wanted me to tell them that I'm nothing but a fake bride."

He jerked his head back to her and saw the anger in her eyes. "Hell, Clare. I didn't think you were stealing it."

She shrugged and turned away. "It's obvious from your face that it means a great deal to you."

"What does a trinket mean when she's not here? When you can't bear to…" *To even look at me*, he meant to say. But he caught the words. "You should keep it. It's not like I'm going to run out and get another wife anytime soon. Or ever."

"I don't want it," she insisted stubbornly. "Not when it's an empty gesture. Not when it comes without…"

"Without what?"

"Without what it truly represents."

Dev's voice rose. "I can't believe we're fighting about that necklace when there's…" He raised his palms and sighed. "I'm sorry, Clare. I'm not myself. Not in this place."

"I get that, Dev, I do." Her expression softened. "I promised myself I'd be polite and calm with you today."

"As opposed to the sweet and tart woman that pushes and prods?" he said with a laugh.

She walked over to the bedroom door and closed it. "Dev, talk to your father please."

"You really want to pick a fight with me today, don't you?"

She frowned, her beautiful blue eyes not leaving his face. "Not at all. But I'm not going to back down from it, if that's what it takes."

Dev gave in. "Fine. Why would you push me to

have a heart-to-heart with the man who crushed me when I was young?"

"Because I think he's finally realized he's made a mistake. Because he doesn't know how to ask you for your forgiveness."

"Why are you on his side, Clare?"

Only when he heard it did Dev realize how pathetic he sounded. How childish. How he seemed to have morphed back into a needy, temperamental pre-teen inside these walls.

Was it this that had been bothering him? That Clare got along so well with his family, with his father? That he…wanted her to be his and no one else's?

She was his. Only his. The first and only woman who'd seen more in him than he himself did.

She came and took hold of one of his hands. Lifted it and pressed her mouth to his knuckles. Cradled his palm to her face. "I'm on your side, Dev. Always."

"Then why do you ask me to do this when you know how impossible I'd find it?"

"Because I care about you." She pressed her hand to his chest, boldly. As if she was staking a claim on his heart. As if she was laying claim to the whole of him. His pulse rushed deafeningly, but the look in her eyes was calm. She was composed and elegant and the most beautiful woman he'd ever seen. "Because I think that talking to him, letting him say his bit…whether it's to ask for forgiveness or to justify his attitude back then… I think it will help you. I think it will finally burn away the resentment and anger that's been building up inside you for so long. Because I think until you face your past and gain closure, there's no possibility of a happy future for you."

"I'm here, aren't I?" he retorted.

"But are you, really? Did you let your brother get close to you? Did you let Diya see the real you? Or did you only come to show off to your father? To prove to him how rich and powerful you've become. To thumb your nose at him. I've spent some time talking to him recently, and for a sixty-five-year-old man stuck inside his own rigid set of values, I think he knows he wronged you and he's really been trying to change."

"Of course he's changed. But only because I've changed, can't you see? I'm not the lazy, useless, rogue he used to call me. I've become something more. I've amassed all this wealth and power and I finally made the family name proud. He can afford to be proud of me now. He can afford to call me his son."

"But it's not just recently, Dev. That's what Deedi was trying to tell you. He's followed your progress for years. Your entire swimming career, your first company, your first takeover, your work with Athleta. He's been proud of you for a very long time now."

The bitterness inside him was so deep and dense that nothing she was saying impacted on it. Dev wanted so badly to shift it. To cleanse himself of the poison. If not for himself, then for her. To be open to whatever it was she was trying to bring into his life. But he couldn't. "It is easy for him to say he's changed, Clare. Easy for him to give me the approval and the love he denied me once."

"But it's you who's denying all those things now, Dev. Don't you see? You're measuring yourself by his standards from back then. You're letting ugly things from the past dictate your present and your future."

A frustrated groan fell from his mouth. He grasped her shoulders. "Why are you forcing this discussion on me?"

"Because I've seen the shadows of loneliness in your eyes these past few days. I've seen how you look at your nieces and nephews, as if you're an ocean away from everyone. I've seen you say no to almost every overture and invitation that Diya and Deedi have made to you. I've seen you shut them all down repeatedly. Hold yourself apart."

"Because I'm angry and hurt and I...want so badly to belong. But I think..." Dev pressed his fingers to his temples, hating the sick churning in his stomach. "I don't know how. I've stayed away for too long. I..."

She wrapped her arms around his waist and

held him, this woman who had a core of steel at her center. "Then take the first step, Dev. Talk to him. Try and sort it out. Make peace with your father. For yourself, if no one else. Despite what he did, if I had one more chance to see my dad, I'd take it."

Dev held her for a few seconds but his breath didn't settle. He felt as if he was standing on the outside again. Not knowing how to read or what to say.

"I can't," he said abruptly, letting Clare go. "I can't open myself up to all that pain again. I can't give him or anyone else the chance to..."

"Hurt you again," Clare finished sadly, stepping back from him.

Dev swallowed and shrugged.

"So what does this mean for us then?" she asked quietly.

"What do you mean?" he asked, feeling like a fool. "It doesn't change anything. This was just another part of our agreement, Clare. This was just you...giving me a hand with getting through some difficult days. Nothing has changed."

She didn't answer. And Dev felt a helplessness that he hadn't known in a long time.

He pulled her to him and she came.

"I want to kiss you," he said, plunging his fingers into her hair. "I need to taste you, sweetheart."

"Yes, please," she whispered.

He felt as if he'd conquered the world. He took her mouth, employing all the skill he possessed to push her to the same sense of desperation he felt. She was sweet and warm, like light in a cave of darkness.

And when he let her go, she looked up at him. Her long fingers cradled his cheek with a tenderness he didn't deserve. "I'm planning to leave for London tonight on the red-eye."

Dev's ferocious scowl told Clare everything she needed to know. She knew that she was pushing him when he wasn't himself. But as she'd already learned, there was no right or wrong time to do this.

To tell the man she loved that she…was an absolute fool for him.

"I'll have the jet ready in an hour or two. We can leave together."

"No." She stepped away from him, feeling as if she was cleaving herself in two. "I'd prefer to go alone. I haven't been to the office in weeks, and Amy and Bea, I know, are wondering where the hell I've got to."

"So I'll be in the way of your reunion with your friends?" he asked harshly.

"No. I just want to get my head on straight." She pressed her hand to his mouth, incapable of not touching him.

He pulled her hand away but didn't let go.

"I don't understand what you're talking about, Clare."

"I've fallen in love with you, Dev." Her hand went to the black bead necklace at her throat. "I… I want this marriage to be real. I want to be Mrs. Kohli. I want this family to be mine as well as yours. More than anything, I want to share my life with you too. Are you happy to modify our arrangement to suit my needs?"

He didn't blink. He simply stood there, staring at her.

Clare laughed bitterly. "Yeah, I didn't think so. This is why I pushed you. Because I know how it feels for past scars to dictate your future. To have been so hurt badly that you close yourself off to everything. Even love. I waited for my dad to come back to me for years, Dev. Decades. You know he never did. You know what he ended up doing to me. You saw what it took for me to come back from it. You restored my faith in human nature just when it was ready to be completely shattered. But I can't wait around like that again for a man to love me. I can't…because it will break me this time. Because I love you so much and you're just not ready for it—if you ever will be. You don't want love in your life, do you? So, yes, I have to go. I have to start putting the pieces of my life back together again. I have to decide who I want to be…next."

Clare walked up to the man who'd become her

entire world in such a short space of time. She kissed his bristly cheek and breathed in the delicious scent of him.

"Loving you has only made my life better, Dev. That will never change," she whispered. "But you have to choose happiness, Dev. With me. You have to decide if I'm worth trusting. If I'm worth taking a chance on. If you can finally let me into your heart."

CHAPTER THIRTEEN

DEV DIDN'T KNOW why he was still there—at his parents' house in California. In this house where he had never felt like he fit.

Derek and Angelina were long gone. Diya and Richard had left for their honeymoon a couple of hours after Clare had left him. His older brother and sister and their boisterous families had left too. His family had all bid him goodbye with a wariness that he knew he was the cause of. Both his sisters had asked why Clare had left so abruptly.

When would he bring her back for a visit?

When was he going to let them throw a party for him and Clare to celebrate their marriage? Had he convinced Clare yet to move to California with him so that they would all be closer together?

As if he were a stranger they couldn't communicate with without the bridge Clare had provided. As if she had...opened up something between him and them again.

As if she'd rekindled a spark in his cold heart.

There were a hundred things requiring his attention, tens of meetings he was missing with each day he didn't leave. And yet he had stayed, a strange lethargy weighing him down.

Instead of that agitated energy he'd felt during the first few days after his return, Dev sensed something different within the house this time. The walls looked brighter. The sight of him in the family portrait above the giant fireplace—the one he'd tried to get out of being included in—suddenly didn't feel like a joke of the worst kind.

As the hours and days passed, he felt as if the house gradually changed around him. As if for the first time in years, he could breathe here. Or was it him who had changed?

Or was it Clare who had made life so much better for him that the past no longer held such significance anymore?

As he sat down in the huge library with the vaulted ceilings and rows and rows of books that had always seemed like alien things forever out of his reach, Dev realized he didn't feel the resentment that had been his childhood companion for so long. He didn't feel caged anymore.

Because now, whichever wing he walked into, whatever nook or corner he looked into, he saw Clare.

He saw her laughing with Diya and Deedi.

He saw her turning bright pink as she tasted

the spicy *pakoda* his nephew had popped into her mouth when she'd been laughing.

He saw her looking up from where she'd been sitting amid all his cousins and relatives on her knees, her lovely, warm gaze finding him wherever he was and smiling at him.

He saw her dragging him through room after room, laughing, asking questions, determined to know all the hijinks he'd gotten into as a mischievous boy. He saw her kissing him, needing him, telling him he was loved with her eyes, her kisses and her generous heart.

But her words…the very words he didn't even know he'd needed to hear so desperately, the very words that were in his own heart…when she'd finally said those words to him out loud, he hadn't been able to hear them.

He hadn't been able to see what it had cost her to say them to him. How far she'd come to be able to trust him, and want him, and…love him.

His father was still there, Dev knew. The palatial mansion meant he and the old man didn't have to cross paths even once during the day if they so pleased. While Papa had rarely approached Dev, he constantly sensed his father's presence, in the weighty silence that seemed to follow him wherever he walked.

In the pregnant hope that filled the very air.

"The house is yours," his father had declared,

the one time Dev had come close enough to him for a conversation.

"I don't want it." The words had risen to Dev's mouth and yet...something had arrested them. No, not something. Someone.

Clare.

"That wife of yours," Papa had continued in his booming voice, "she will like the house, I think. She will want to raise a family here with you."

Dev had looked up, stunned. For the first time in his life, it seemed his father and he had been thinking along the same lines. The picture of her, in this house, with him, was such a clear image that Dev hadn't been capable of responding.

The two of them together in this house, building a family together...

And for the first time in years, Dev saw himself fitting into this house again. Fitting in with his family. Fitting in with who he'd wanted to be all his life—a man worthy of love.

And Clare had made it all possible by simply loving him.

By giving him what he wasn't even sure he'd earned.

"Who the hell are you?"

If Dev didn't feel as if his heart was lodged in his throat, if he hadn't felt like a total idiot, he'd have laughed at the two women who blocked his way as he walked into the offices of The London Connection.

One tall and elegant, the other a little shorter, with strawberry blond hair—they looked like sentinels guarding the gate against him. Guarding their best friend.

A part of him found relief in the fact that Clare had these women to support her. That she wasn't alone. That she...

"I'm here to see Clare," he said, trying to hide the impatience he felt.

"We heard you the first time. Our question was who are you?" asked the blonde.

Dev pushed his hand through his hair. "You damn well know who I am. I'm your best friend's husband."

Shock seemed to quiet them for once. Until he heard one muttering away and the other one squealing. Something like, "Oh, my God, he's here!"

"I don't think you should be here," the taller one said.

"Wait, Bea, we don't know that. She might want to see him. You know what shape she's been in since she returned. Also, he's our biggest client right now."

Before they drove Dev completely crazy, Clare appeared behind them. Peeking out of the back door, leading to a separate office.

"What's going on...?"

Her words fell away as she straightened. Wariness shone in her eyes as she tucked a lock of dark brown hair behind her ear. "Hey, Dev."

Dev swallowed, trying to dislodge the torrent of emotion that seemed to crawl upward from his chest into his throat. He didn't say anything in the end. Just nodded at her. Stared at her hungrily.

She looked a little gaunt but elegant in a white blouse and black skirt. She looked lovely and fierce and his breath came back in a rush, as if he'd been merely functioning until now, instead of living.

"I didn't know you were coming to London." Her tone made it clear she'd have been three continents away if she had. "Did I miss something on the calendar? I thought we'd finished all the PR for Athleta."

"No. That's all wrapped up," he finally said. "I'm sure you've seen the articles. I'm now being praised as a twenty-first-century model CEO."

"With most of his female fans crying over the fact that he secretly married his English wife," added the one called Bea.

Clare flushed. Her arms wound around herself in a gesture of defensiveness that tugged at Dev's heart. "It's okay, Bea. He'll be back on the market soon enough." Her blue gaze pinned him. "In fact, now that you're here, maybe we can finalize—"

"No, I won't," Dev said loudly. Enough was enough!

"You won't what, Mr. Kohli?" asked the blonde who must be Amy.

"I'm not going back on the market," he snapped. "For anything." And before she could shoot him down with another question, he caught up to her. "I want to talk to you in private."

Her breath quickened as he neared her. "I don't see what we have to say to each other. I'm not interested in playing Mr. Kohli's adoring wife anymore."

"No? I thought you were pretty damn good at it," he said, grinning. Gaining a little of his confidence back. He'd have to beg, yes, but she'd forgive him. She loved him. And the one thing he knew about Clare was that she didn't give her heart away easily.

And once she did, she was never going to take it back again. God, he'd been so foolish.

The woman he'd married was not the flaky type. She wasn't going to kick him out of her life just because he'd been slow to see what was right in front of his eyes.

"Did you get the profile of that last magazine interview I sent you?"

Her blue eyes grew huge in her face. "I opened it just now... I...it's a brave, big move publicizing your dyslexia like that."

Dev smiled. "I didn't do it to be brave or big.

I did it because I realized you were right. I was still measuring myself by someone else's standards. And failing. In truth, telling the world I'm dyslexic is a selfish act, Clare. Really, I'm doing it to prove to myself and to you that… I choose happiness. That I choose love. That I choose… you. I love you, sweetheart. I want a future with you, if you'll still have me. I'll even give up the monstrous, gigantic, oversized yacht if it means my tomorrows are filled with you…"

Tears filled her eyes and fell across her cheeks. She looked so stricken that Dev felt a flicker of fear.

"Do you still not trust me?" he muttered hoarsely.

She shook her head, and then she was throwing herself into his arms. "I trusted you from that first night. You gave me my heart back, Dev." A world of joy filled her eyes. "You were just so determined to stay a bachelor."

"But that was before you stormed into my life, Clare." He kissed her temple and held her as she trembled in his arms.

Dev heard a couple of masculine voices behind him but ignored them. The only one who mattered to him, the only person he ever wanted to see was here in front of him.

"I love you. I think I fell in love with you when I found you sleeping in my closet. You're so brave and sweet and I can't imagine what my life would be like if you hadn't come storming into it, Clare.

Forgive me for being a foolish man. For not seeing what you were giving me, sweetheart." He opened the top couple of buttons on his shirt and there lay the necklace she'd left behind on his nightstand.

"I want you to be my wife, Clare. Forever and ever. My father has been trying to give me the family home, but if you don't like the idea, I want you to help me pick a house for us wherever you want to live. I want you to have a big family with me. Because I know that's what you've always wanted. I want you to teach our children how to be strong and brave like you. I want you to give me a chance to love you like you've always deserved to be loved, darling. And I promise I'll never again keep you waiting. Not another minute, not another second."

And then she was burying her face in his neck and murmuring through her tears.

"I do love you, Dev. With all my heart. I…"

Dev kissed her quiet. "Shh…sweetheart, no more tears. I'm here. I'll always be here for you."

EPILOGUE

"Do we have to change the name of our company now that we have offices on two continents?"

Clare looked up to find her friend Bea considering the question thoughtfully, the way she did everything else. Her husband Ares was sitting by her, his arm around her on the couch. Amy and Luca, on the other hand, sat squashed up on the opposite recliner together, still arguing over where they were going to spend Christmas.

She smiled as strong arms came around her waist and she was pulled against a hard body. Warmth exploded in her blood as the familiar scent of her husband enveloped her.

"Are you going to answer Bea's question or are you just going to grin like a fool?" Amy demanded, laughing at what Clare was sure was a blissful look on her face.

"Luca, please advise your wife not to call mine a fool."

Luca grinned while Amy continued. "Well, your wife is the CEO of our company and since she's made the executive decision of ditching us and moving to California to open the US branch of our business, Bea and I have been wondering."

Clare straightened, hearing the hint of uncertainty in Amy's voice. When she looked at Bea, she found the same.

Her friends weren't worried about the business or their share of it. But The London Connection had brought them together when they had nothing else in the world. Nothing but each other.

"Of course, we're not going to change the name," Clare said, clearing her throat. "I'm just one flight away from you. And remember, ladies, we're all about the modern woman."

"What Clare means, Amy," Bea chipped in, while smiling at Ares, "is that Ares and Luca and Dev know better than to expect that we'll put them before the business."

Amy laughed and Clare joined in. She couldn't believe all three of them had met and fallen in love with such wonderful men.

With Dev by her side and her friends near enough to see regularly, she finally had everything she had ever wanted—love and a big family and a place to belong.

* * * * *

Wrapped up in the drama of Tara Pammi's
The Playboy's "I Do" Deal?
*You're sure to enjoy the first and second
instalments in the Signed, Sealed... Seduced
miniseries*

Ways to Ruin a Royal Reputation
by Dani Collins
Cinderella's Night in Venice
by Clare Connolly
Available now!

And catch these other stories by Tara Pammi!

An Innocent to Tame the Italian
A Deal to Carry the Italian's Heir
The Flaw in His Marriage Plan
Claiming His Bollywood Cinderella
The Surprise Bollywood Baby

Available now!